DIARY OF AN 8-BIT VILLAGER WARRIOR

Published in French under the title *Journal d'un Noob (Guerrier) Tome I*
© 2016 by 404 éditions, an imprint of Édi8, Paris, France
Text © 2015 by Cube Kid, Illustration © 2016 by Saboten

Andrews McMeel Publishing
a division of Andrews McMeel Universal
1130 Walnut Street, Kansas City, Missouri 64106
www.andrewsmcmeel.com

16 17 18 19 20 RR2 10 9 8 7 6 5 4 3

ISBN: 978-1-4494-8005-9

Library of Congress Control Number: 2016933974

Made by:
RR Donnelley Printing Company Ltd.
Address and location of manufacturer:
1009 Sloan Street
Crawfordsville, IN 47933
3rd Printing — 7/22/16

ATTENTION: SCHOOLS AND BUSINESSES
Andrews McMeel books are available at quantity discounts with bulk purchase for educational, business, or sales promotional use. For information, please e-mail the Andrews McMeel Publishing Special Sales Department: specialsales@amuniversal.com.

• CUBE KID •

DIARY OF AN 8-BIT VIL~~LAGER~~ WARRIOR

Illustrations by
Saboten

Andrews McMeel
Publishing®
a division of Andrews McMeel Universal

In memory of Lola Salines (1986–2015),
founder of 404 éditions and editor of this series,
who lost her life in the November 2015 attacks on Paris.
Thank you for believing in me.

– Cube Kid

Squeak?
Squeeeee?
Cheeeeeee-ehhhhhhh!

These annoying sounds woke me up in the middle of the night. **The sounds of a spider. On top of my house.**

It must have wandered into our **village** after sunset. And decided that the roof over my bedroom was a cool place to hang out.

Screeee?
Squeak-squeak-squeak?

I covered my head with my pillow. It didn't help. Soon, I could hear a slime moving around out there. **Blap, blap, blap.** It almost sounded like someone was beating the ground with a big dead fish. Then a **zombie** joined in with its horrible moaning.

"What are they doing out there?" I muttered to myself. "Are they trying to start a band or something?!"

Hurrrrrr.

(In case you don't know, "hurrrrrrr" is the sound a villager makes when thinking. Or irritated. And right now, I'm super irritated. The mobs can't get to us in our homes, so they make noises all night just to annoy us.)

1

Still lying in bed, I simply stared at the ceiling and made that sound.

Hurrrrrrr, hurrrrrrr, hurrrrrrr . . .

(I'd trade two hundred emeralds for something that could go over my ears and block that awful noise. A pillow just isn't enough.)

Sigh.

This is the life of a villager. We're helpless against the mobs. Monsters, that is. They arrive almost every night, and there's nothing we can do except hide in our little houses. I wish we could fight them off. Unfortunately, villagers aren't allowed to become warriors. The village elders say being a warrior is too dangerous. The only thing we can do is **farm, farm, farm. Harvest, harvest, harvest**. And stay indoors all night until the sun comes up.

Still, even if we don't have any **warriors**, I've met some. They sometimes visit our village, Villagetown. They never stay for very long, though. Just long enough to rest up and trade. They don't look like us at all. They have **swords** and **armor**. And they go exploring. And adventuring.

I sometimes talk to one of them. His name is **Steve**. He's a pretty cool guy. A few weeks ago, he killed a couple of **zombies** in our village. My family was especially thankful for that. One of those zombies had just stood right outside the front door looking in, mouth hanging open, making the loudest grunting sounds.

Sometimes, I wish I could be like **Steve**. He gets to run around doing whatever he wants. Every morning he must wake up and think, "Oh, **what will I do today? Slay some mobs? Explore some temples? Find some treasure?**"

Meanwhile, the most interesting thing I do is collect seeds . . .

I often wonder:
Does Steve have a village? Where does he come from?

The next time I speak with him, I'll have to ask.

Anyway, if I actually defeated a mob some day, none of the other kids could call me a **noob** anymore. According to most of them, I'm just a noob worthy of my name:

Runt!!!

As you can imagine, I get a lot of grief over this name . . . Especially from **Max**. He's so annoying. He always says I'm useless, no good. He wants to be a librarian, and he thinks he knows everything because he's read nearly every book in Villagetown. That really doesn't mean much at all, though, because a lot of books in our village totally stink. I mean, most of Max's so-called **worldly** knowledge comes from a series titled *The Adventures of Cow the Cow*.

Whatever. If I ever become a warrior, he'll be saluting me. And, after he salutes me, he'll be shining my boots, and addressing me as "Sir," or perhaps "**Commander**," and asking me how many slices of pumpkin pie I'd like for lunch.

* * *

Okay, so, our village is boring at times.

Here's another thing I don't like about it: **the trading**.

For example, if you want some cookies, well, it's not like you just go down to the store, slam three emeralds onto the counter, and call it a done deal. No, no, no. In reality, you walk into the store, hoping the guy selling the cookies is having a good day. If he's not, he's going to "**hurrrrr**" for what seems like forever as he thinks about a "**fair price**"— and the whole time, your stomach's rumbling, and you're telling yourself things like, "Maybe I should just have a raw potato instead."

 In fact, I had to spend a total of ten emeralds on this diary you're reading right now.

That librarian totally ripped me off. My mom gave me those emeralds for lunch at school. **If she found out that I spent a week's worth of lunch emeralds on a diary . . .**

But I guess the librarian was nice compared to that blacksmith a few days ago. He wanted thirty emeralds for a pair of leather boots, and the boots weren't even in new condition.

Seriously, would someone actually pay that much?

4

Then again, my friend Stump said he once sold a moldy potato to a warrior for five emeralds. **I guess that warrior was really hungry . . .**

* * *

I have to watch out for more than just traders, too. Some of the villager kids are real jerks. Especially that kid **Max**. He's always telling these unbelievable stories. Well, some kids believe him.

Max likes scaring anyone he can. The other day, he was telling some kids about a monster called the **"poo screamer."** Supposedly, a **poo screamer** is a special type of **creeper**.

Creepers are green, of course, because they're made out of leaves. But a poo screamer is brown because it's . . .

Um . . .
Made out of poo.

You really **don't** want to be around when one of these things explodes.

When it attacks, **it doesn't hiss** like normal. It makes a loud gurgling sound. Or so Max says.

Of course, Max just made it up. I know that. But a few little kids totally fell for it.

While those kids were playing in the street, Max hid behind a nearby house. Then he made the sound a **poo screamer** supposedly makes.

"Graagraaagggurrrrggggggg-fttttt‼⁄"

It terrified some of those kids. From what I heard, they wouldn't go near a bathroom for days after. They didn't want the poo screamer to get them.

Yeah. Welcome to my life.
Irritating mobs.
Greedy librarians.

And Max.

Last night, **I had a crazy dream**.

Our village had warriors, and I was one of them.

I looked **endermen** straight in the eye.

I deflected **skeleton** arrows with my bare hands.

I mowed down **zombies** like a farmer harvesting beetroots.

Finally, I punched a **creeper** so hard, it bounced off the ground and flew up into the sun, where it exploded, making the sun brighter. The brighter sun burned up **the rest of the skeletons and zombies.**

Yeah.

That's the kind of **warrior** I want to be.

But that was just a dream. The reality is . . . school is starting on Monday, and I just turned twelve.

<u>**Twelve.**</u> That's the age when villagers stop being kids and learn a profession. A lot of other kids are into subjects like **farming, crafting,** and **building** . . . but **combat** is my favorite subject. I just wish our school had a few combat classes. **I don't want to be a blacksmith or a butcher.** Maybe a priest? Or maybe I can just run away and <u>**be like Steve.**</u>

No, how could I run away? **I love my mom too much.** My dad's pretty cool, too. Of course, he wants me to become a farmer like him.

It's hard being a farmer, by the way.

People can just walk up and steal your crops. That happened today. Some weird guy came into our village and started taking our carrots. My dad tried to stop him, and the guy hit my dad with his stone pickaxe. I was really angry. But the **iron golem** nearby was way angrier. The golem punched that guy so hard, he dropped his pickaxe and ran away.

I sold that pickaxe to a blacksmith for three emeralds . . .

I guess I'm learning, huh?

The mobs attacked again last night.

Why would anyone want to attack such a beautiful place?

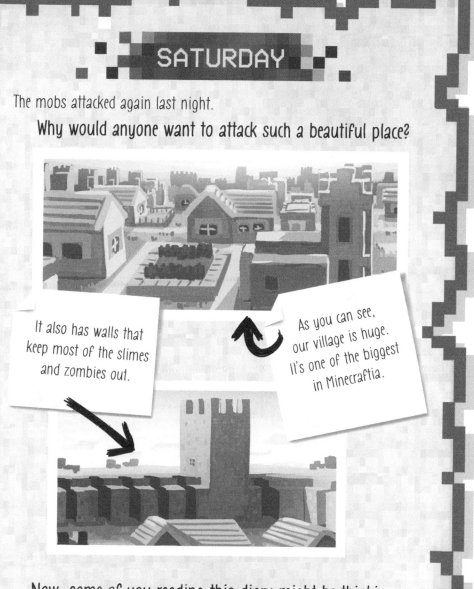

As you can see, our village is huge. It's one of the biggest in Minecraftia.

It also has walls that keep most of the slimes and zombies out.

Now, some of you reading this diary might be thinking:
"Wait!! Villages don't have walls!!!"

This isn't just any village, though, it's Villagetown. And it wasn't us who came up with idea for the wall. **Steve** taught us how to build it.

Besides, if you were a villager, what would you do?

Would you seriously not want to build a wall? We're not **stupid**, you know. **Most of us, anyway.** The mayor won't let us fight the mobs directly, but we can still defend ourselves. Not that it matters too much . . . Even with a stone wall surrounding our village, the mobs still get in, as you can see from the other night.

The mobs around here are really, really smart.

Don't believe me?
Let me tell you about what the mobs did last night.

They came up with a way to get a **bunch of slimes** over the wall. It's a nasty little trick that shows just how clever the mobs can be.

We're calling it the creeper bomb!!!

I'll try drawing it to give you an idea.

Crazy,
right? !!!

BOOM

This is how it worked:

Basically, **slimes** piled onto a **creeper. And boom!**
The creeper exploded. The blast threw the slimes high into the sky.
Some went over the wall, into the city. Of course, **the explosion killed
the slimes**. Here's the thing,
though: **When a slime dies,
it splits into smaller
slimes.**

a rain of baby
slimes, into
the city.

So the result of a
creeper bomb is

BOOM

11

I was outside when it happened. As I looked up, a baby slime fell from the sky . . . and landed right on my face. It died from the fall. But I was drenched in disgusting ooze. **Also, I coughed up a slimeball. Gack.**

I'm probably going to have nightmares tonight. **Don't laugh at me.** I mean, how would you feel if a **baby slime splattered all over you?** You probably wouldn't be very happy.

Then, as luck would have it, my mom made **mushroom stew** for lunch. **Really?** Was that some kind of joke? I get attacked by a **slime**, and she's making me mushroom stew? I wouldn't eat it.

I couldn't. I just couldn't.

Anyway, you just wouldn't believe how creative the mobs are. They're getting smarter. They're cooperating. And that creeper bomb is just **one** of their cheap tactics.

There's also the "zombie ladder," where zombies form a staircase next to the wall.

the zombie ladder

Or the "spider elevator," where spiders carry other mobs up and over the wall.

Maybe you're thinking:

"Wait! Mobs don't do those things!
Mobs don't work together!!/"

All I can really say is . . . just come to my village. You'll find out. The life of a villager isn't easy in these parts.

It's humiliating, the way they treat us. I really wish we could fight back. Then we wouldn't have to suffer anymore . . .

However, there is a **rumor** going around that maybe, **just maybe**, some of the students can enter **warrior training** this year. I'm not getting my hopes up, though.

Okay, I have to go take another bath.
I've already taken one,
but I still smell like slime.

School starts tomorrow.

I'm a little nervous. I still haven't put much thought into my **profession**.

This morning, I had to go gather seeds again. **Sigh**. My exciting life.
I took a stick with me. I pretended the stick was a sword. The tall clumps
of grass were skeletons. The short
grass was spiders.

Pathetic, I know.

After thirty minutes of
attacking the grass for their
seeds, **I saw Steve.**

As he approached, I
remembered the question I'd wanted
to ask him. **"Hey, where do you
come from, anyway? A village?"**

"Village?" He shook his head.

**"No, no.
I'm . . . from another world."**

Another world? What was he talking about? I must have looked at him kind of strangely, because he sighed.

"Whatever. None of the other villagers believe me. Why should you?"

For a second, I decided to just play along. I thought maybe he was joking with me or something.

"Okay," I said. "Then what's the name of your, um, **world?**"

"**Earth.**"

"Earth? That's **a strange name**, isn't it? How did you get here?"

"I don't know," he said. "I can't remember much. One second, I was there. And then, I was here. But that was months ago."

Well, he didn't look like any of us villagers. Maybe he really did come from another world. When I looked at him, I saw a kind of sadness in his eyes. I wanted to cheer him up.

"I hope you find your way back home," I said. "Your parents must miss you."

"Thanks," he said, and paused. "Wait. So . . . you actually believe me?"

I nodded. "Of course. You saved our village, after all. You showed us how to build that wall. **Thanks.**"

"No problem," he said. "The mobs around here are pretty hardcore. Figured you guys could use a hand."

I nodded again. For a moment, neither of us said anything.

". . ."

". . ."

Then I spoke up.

"Steve? Do you think a villager could ever **become a warrior?**"

Steve beamed like the square sun.

"The way you were slaying that grass earlier," he said, "yeah. I don't see why not."

"But our elders won't allow it," I said. "They say it's too dangerous."

"Well, sometimes, you have to fight back," Steve said. "That's part of life, **you know?**"

I sighed. "The only thing I know is watering crops. And feeding **chickens and pigs**."

Steve put a hand upon my shoulder.

"**You're not missing out on anything**," he said. "Trust me on this one. Three days ago, I was sleeping in a dirt hole and eating raw fish. Sound amazing to you?"

"Not exactly."

"So appreciate what you have."

"Maybe you're right. **Hurrrrrr.**"

"By the way," he said, "did you start school yet?"

"Nope."

"Hmm. Let me show you a few tricks on crafting."

And so, for the rest of the day, **I learned a few things from Steve**. While we were crafting tools, he asked if he could borrow the wooden stick I'd been playing with earlier. I told him it'd be his for the low, low price of just twenty emeralds . . .

Yeah.
I'm definitely learning.

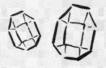

I had my first day of school **today.**

The Villager School of Minecraft and Warriory

It wasn't so bad.

Max saw me writing in this diary, though. Since he plans to be a librarian, he wanted to take a look at it. I didn't let him, of course. If he read anything about himself, he'd find a way to get revenge. He'd probably tell all the other kids something involving me, **diapers,** and a **poo screamer**.

A couple of villager parents were talking nearby in old villager speak:

" . . . rurr . . . hurrr-hurr, rhurrr . . . rurr?
. . . rhurrhurrhuurrrrrr . . ."

First thing in the morning, **assistants** gave students their schedules.
Here are my classes:

```
* * * MORNING * * *
        CRAFTING
  ESSENTIAL WALL BUILDING
   ANTI-CREEPER DEFENSE
     TRICKING ZOMBIES
     ESCAPING ZOMBIES

* * * AFTERNOON * * *
  ANTI-SKELETON DEFENSE
     TRADING BASICS
  ADVANCED WHEAT FARMING
```

Hurrr.

I'm not really into crafting, to be honest. I'd take farming over
crafting, anyway.

Mostly because my parents have already taught me the basics of
farming, so I feel comfortable with it.

At some point, **the village elders showed up at our school—** along with the mayor himself. <u>**That meant something important**</u> <u>**was happening, obviously.**</u> And when the mayor started giving one of his speeches, talking about mobs, my heart started to soar.

"We need to adapt," the mayor said. "The mobs are getting smarter. Stronger. They're working together. **So we need to start fighting back.**"

"We know many of you have been asking about this," said another elder. "We realize we can't just hide in our homes forever . . ."

The head teacher stepped forward.

"And so, what this means is . . . **the top five students** this year . . . will have the opportunity **to be warriors** . . ."

A few gasps spread through the crowd of students. Then hushed excitement. No one could believe it. Including myself. **The rumors were true?**

At the end of the school year, the **top five students** can choose to become **warriors?**

It was as if my prayers had been answered. (I did pray, sometimes. Our village has a church, you know.)

However, there are **150 students this year** . . . The competition will be extremely tough. **Max** is most likely going to try, just so he can brag about it, and so will **Pebble**, a kid who is **arguably worse than Max**. Actually, most of the students will probably try out. Wielding a sword? Wearing armor? **That's just too cool.**

This year, the elders are actually giving students a reason to do well in school.

After the speech, I talked things over with my best friend, **Stump**. He was **freaking out** about the whole thing even more than I was. An hour later, we had to take a bunch of tests. They were simple tests, like crafting sticks and planting wheat. But it was all timed. After the examination was over, the teachers gave each student a "**performance sheet.**"

Here's my
performance sheet.

RUNT'S
PERFORMANCE :
FARMING   6%
BUILDING   0%
CRAFTING   3%
LEVEL 3

How
depressing.

I didn't do too well on building, apparently. My mind was wandering during the whole examination. I couldn't stop thinking about the possibility of actually becoming a **sword-wielding, mob-crushing cool guy** like **Steve**.

At villager school they assign you to a certain level based on your test results.

Level 1 is a total noob.
Level 100
means total competence in all fields.

I tested out at level 3. That's not too bad. **Stump's** still only level 1, and **Sara**—a girl I'm friends with—is level 2. So I thought I was cool being a third-level student on the first day of school. Then **Max** showed off his performance sheet.

He was level 5.
Wow!!!

Would he ever stop being so annoying?

As I stared at his sheet, he glanced at mine.

And laughed. Of course.

"If you ever became a warrior," he said, "I wonder what they'd call you? **The Noob Lord?**"

"More like the **Baby Police**," I said. "I mean, someone's got to keep your **wimp levels** in check."

"Whatever."

Max

He handed my sheet back to me. **"When I hit level 100** and you're still at level 10, I'll let you be my assistant. **How's that? Hurrr!"**

I glared at him. **"Moo."**

Max's cheeks turned red. *The Adventures of Cow the Cow* is **practically for babies**, yet it's Max's favorite. I saw him reading it a couple weeks ago. He was real secretive about it. **He doesn't want anyone to know.**

"Rrrrrrurrrrrg!"

Max walked away without saying anything else.

When I found my friend **Stump**, he looked angry. He was staring down at his performance sheet. I looked at my own sheet, also feeling a little glum.

"**Level 1**," Stump said. "**Level 1!!** I'm not even a second-level student!! Am I really so bad?!"

"Not at all," I said. "You'll catch up. Your parents are **bakers**, so you know some stuff about crafting, right? And my parents are **farmers**. We can help each other out, huh?"

He nodded, then crumpled up his performance sheet and threw it onto the floor as hard as he could. "Maybe I don't have a chance at being in the top five, but I'm not going to be humiliated like this!! **I'm going to be at least level 50!!**"

I totally agreed with him. From this point on, I had a clear goal. When I hit **level 100**, I'll hand my performance sheet to Max. Then I'll say . . . **um** . . . well, I'll say something witty. **I'm sure of it**.

**Maybe I should think about what
I'm going to say when that day comes.**

Today, in farming class, we had to learn how to take **care of sheep**.

My family only has **pigs** and **chickens**, so I'd never really dealt with **sheep** before, but they had one thing in common with the farm animals I knew—they'll stare at you in a **creepy way** whenever you're holding food. Still, I find sheep to be the creepiest, for some reason.

MISTER, GIVE US SOME WHEAT.

How can you say no?

Then we learned how to shear sheep. I didn't realize it until now, but sheared sheep **look really, really strange**.

25

Almost like dogs or something

I honestly wonder what a hungry, sheared sheep would look like. I'm not sure if I even want to imagine it.

Hurrrrrr.

Sheep scare me now. **Hooray**.

* * *

Later, I found out that my **Tricking Zombies** class was changed to **Mining Basics**. **Max** is in that class.

Hurrrgggggurgurgurgurgurgg.
Gurg.
Urgurg.

Tricking Zombies sounded like a really fun class. But then, anything is better than **mining**.

Let me tell you, swinging a pickaxe is the hardest thing **of all time**. I don't want to be a miner. After just one hour, my arms felt like **dead slime**. But Stump is in that class, too, so it wasn't all bad. We collected a ton of cobblestone. We weren't supposed to get so much. Our teacher didn't even know what to do with all of it. I think we've got enough for a new village.

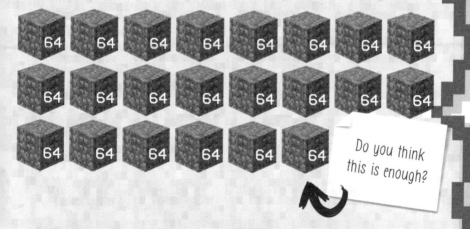

Do you think this is enough?

Okay, so we didn't get **THAT** much. But still. We mined a lot.

Of course, **before we even started mining**, the teachers told us about the "golden rule."

I'd heard it **many** times before, but I guess the teachers thought that it was necessary to repeat during the first week of school.

Okay. Let's test your knowledge.

The golden rule is:

A) Eat lots of cookies.

B) Always hug creepers.

C) Never dig straight down.

D) Thermonuclear corncobs.

Which one, **hurr**? You probably know. It's easy. The answer is . . .

A) Eat lots of cookies**!!!**

Just kidding . . . Well, that's what the answer should be. **But it's not.** It's **C)** never dig straight down. **I guess bad things happen when you dig straight down. Very bad things.**

Like what happened to the zombie who had a craving for **diamonds** instead of **brains.**

The legendary zombie miner. He only wanted to eat diamonds. He ended up eating lava instead.

Oh. I almost forgot. This is really embarrassing . . . **maybe I shouldn't even write about it** . . .

I broke my pickaxe while mining today, and forgot to repair it **quickly enough**.

Hurrrrrrg.

So of course **Max** saw it. He laughed at me again. Naturally.

"Hey, Runt," he said. "You should learn to be **more careful**."

"Good tip," I said. "I was just about to be super careless. I was like, 'Hurrrgggggggg, I'm SO not going be to careful right now.'"

Max shrugged. "Just trying to help out. Wouldn't want you to end up like **Spike**. He wasn't careful, either."

"Ugh, another one of your stories," I said, rolling my eyes. "Okay. Let's hear it. **What happened to Spike?**"

And so, **Max** told me the story of a **villager named Spike**.

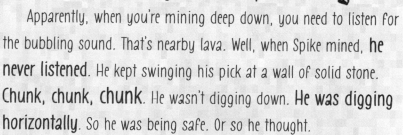

Apparently, when you're mining deep down, you need to listen for the bubbling sound. That's nearby lava. Well, when Spike mined, **he never listened**. He kept swinging his pick at a wall of solid stone. **Chunk, chunk, chunk**. He wasn't digging down. **He was digging horizontally**. So he was being safe. Or so he thought.

Sadly, his little tunnel broke into the side of an underground lava lake. The lava splashed out, and all over him. I guess he barely had time to **scream**. When the other miners came to save him, there was nothing left of him. Just bubbling lava. Oh, and his boots.

I never wanted to be a miner, but hearing Max's story made me not want to be a miner even more.

Backbreaking work?
Check.

Possibility of taking a lava bath?
Check.

There has to be a way out of this. What if I said mining is against my religion? Or that I'm allergic to pickaxes? No, I don't think the teachers will believe any of that . . .

Hey, help me out here!

We had a special **building class** today. At first, they just went on about the **super easy stuff.** Stuff even I knew.

Like how it's a really good idea to put a **crafting table and a furnace** next to each other. Who doesn't know that? They're made for one another.

Aww,
so cute!

Then, it was fun time. We got to work on **building a house.** The teachers said to be creative. So I had the idea of building a furnace house. **Awesome, huh?** Stump thought so, too. So we decided to work on this little project together. After all, it gave us something to do with our **mountain of cobblestone**.

Our furnace house

I mean, why NOT build a **furnace house?**

We had **so much cobblestone**. Plus we could use multiple furnaces to speed up cooking. Come on, why not? You could cook **chicken** in one furnace, **steak** in another, and smelt **iron ore** in a third. The possibilities were just endless. Again, **why not?**

However, our teachers didn't think it was such a great idea . . . They said it was ridiculous. **Pointless, they said. Pointless!** As if. But the teachers insisted.

"You don't need so **many furnaces**," one of them said.

"Also," said another, "it looks a bit **ugly**."

Blah, blah, blah.

It's not fair!!!

Some girls built a few mushroom houses, and the teachers **praised them**!

"Oh! What **lovely** little mushroom cottages!"

"So **cute!**"

"So **wonderful!**"

"**Breathtaking,** really."

"'**Marvelous'** would be the word I'd use, personally."

A mushroom house? Seriously?

Ugh!

I was a little angry. In **our furnace house**, you could cook **thousands of steaks** at the same time. If some guy came over to your house, and that guy was like, "I need to cook one thousand steaks. Right now. Absolutely right now. These big juicy steaks cannot wait. Cannot. I must cook one thousand steaks as fast as possible." You'd be able to say: **"One thousand? Is that all?"**

Now, maybe it's the rare occasion that someone would actually come over to your house and ask to cook one thousand steaks. But hey, with a furnace house, you'll **totally be prepared** for that. Can those girls say the same thing about their fancy little mushroom houses? **Nope.**

And if you found your furnace house to be a little too dark at night? **No problem.** Just pop a wood block into a furnace. **Bam.** You now have a cozy little glow. Would that be possible in <u>mushroom houses?</u> Nope.

I really wish those teachers could have seen how **awesome** our furnace house really was. There was no use dwelling on our **loss**, though.

So Stump and I decided to just build a **normal house.** Small, simple, wooden. What could the teachers possibly say about a house like that? **A lot,** apparently.

I couldn't believe their responses:

"Boring," they said.

"Too **plain.**"

"Who hasn't seen a **wooden** house before?"

One of them even sighed. "Do try to be a little **more imaginative** next time, huh, boys?"

What, a furnace house **wasn't cool enough?!**

But then I had another idea. If the teachers liked the girls' mushroom houses so much, why not build a <u>mushroom CASTLE?</u>

We went to work on it immediately.

Behold, our masterpiece

Our **mushroom castle** had:

- Eight rooms.
- A spiral staircase leading upstairs.
- A back deck with a table and chairs, all made out of mushroom blocks.

It took **us over an hour** to build that thing.

I know what you're probably thinking. That maybe our **mushroom castle** looks a little sloppy. We're not master builders yet, okay? Do you know how hard it is to line up eight giant mushrooms into the shape of a castle? **Super hard.** Probably on the same level of difficulty as **mining obsidian with your fists.**

And do you know what a teacher said to us?

"Now boys . . . you shouldn't be copying those girls. Come up with your own ideas, okay?"

Whatever!!!

Even **feeding sheep** was better than this.
I'm done for today.

I'm still sad and angry about what the teachers said about our **mushroom castle.**

I don't want to write today.

Hurrrrrr.

We had an extra class after school. Every Friday, we have to take a special class on mobs.

It's called Mob Defense.

Today, we started with zombies.

The first thing they taught us about zombies is: A zombie in daytime can be **more dangerous than at night**.

The flaming hug attack of doooom

When a zombie is on fire from the sun . . . it will try to hug you before it dies. That's how much they hate living people. That's how **evil** the mobs are. Honestly, it was a little scary hearing about it. I mean, normal zombies? **Scary.**

But a **burning zombie**? It knows it's going to die. And it will do anything it can to take you with it. It wants nothing more than to wrap its little claws around you. The thought of being hugged by a burning **zombie** and catching on fire . . . **gosh.**

I was getting a little afraid.

Even scarier was what they taught us about a **special type of creeper.**

Apparently, when a **creeper** gets struck by lightning, it **glows blue.** That's called a **"charged creeper."**

Its **blast** is stronger than **TNT.** A charged creeper is the stuff of nightmares. I'll admit, learning about **burning zombies** and **charged creepers** made me think twice about becoming a warrior.

The posters on the school walls didn't help, either. Like this one:

DO NOT LOOK CHARGED
CREEPERS IN THE EYE.
DO NOT ATTACK THEM.

RUN!

And don't stop.

I didn't even know about **charged creepers** until today. **And they're real**. Not imaginary like Max's "**poo screamer**."

So basically, I'll never go **walking around** in a **thunderstorm** ever again.

But flaming zombies and charged creepers aren't even the **most dangerous** mobs, according to the teachers. Skeletons are among the **deadliest**. Mostly because of their range. And when one of their arrows hits you, it knocks you back. If you're standing near a pool of lava when that happens, well . . . **bye-bye**. You'll be joining **Spike**.

To illustrate how dangerous skeletons are, there was this poster:

BEWARE OF SKELETONS!
OR THIS COULD BE YOU.

He's going to be okay, right?

Suddenly, **being a warrior** didn't seem like such a **glamorous** job anymore.

Maybe I should just be a **blacksmith**? That seems like a safe profession.

Am I afraid? Maybe I don't have what it takes to be a **true warrior** . . . A real warrior would never be afraid. Especially not from a poster on a wall.

Well, it's normal to be scared
from time to time, right?
I'm only twelve, after all.

There aren't any classes on Saturdays. So this morning, I hung out with **Steve** again. He helped me **craft a sword.** My very first. I wasn't allowed to make one in Crafting Basics.

Holding it in my hands, the feeling was **unbelievable**.

The stuff of legends

I know, I know, it's only a **wooden sword.**
Hey, I had to start somewhere, right?

Steve crafted a **practice dummy** and I swung my sword at it until half of its durability was gone.

After that, I asked Steve **something that's been on my mind.**

"Hey, Steve. Are you . . . afraid?"

"Afraid?" He blinked. **"Afraid of what?** Mobs?"

" . . "
" . . . "

"Yeah."

"Of course," he said. He paused for a moment. Then he stepped closer. "Actually, you're really going to think I'm crazy if I tell you this, but . . . **I've died in this world before.**"

Died?

What was he talking about?

I didn't understand.

So Steve told me the whole **incredible story**. When he first arrived in our world, he was in a desert. He eventually left that desert and found a forest, where a **creeper** snuck up on him. He heard a hissing sound behind him, turned around, saw the creeper, and—**Boom!** That was the end of Steve.

Except it wasn't. What happened next was really strange.

He says everything went **red**, then **black**. Then he woke up in the very same desert he had originally appeared in.

As I listened to his story, I didn't know what to make of it. **Was Steve telling the truth?**

Not only is he from another world, but . . . **he's immortal as well?** If what he said is true, it means he can become a really good warrior. **A legendary warrior.**

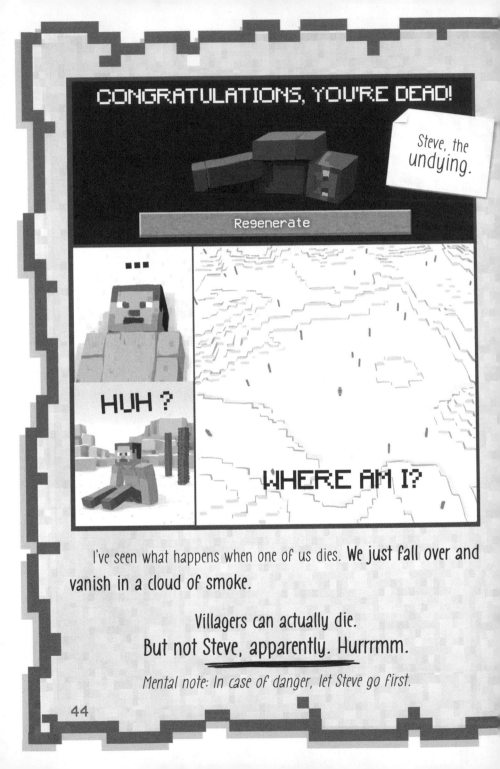

I've seen what happens when one of us dies. We just fall over and vanish in a cloud of smoke.

Villagers can actually die.
But not Steve, apparently. Hurrrmm.

Mental note: In case of danger, let Steve go first.

Wow. I've been writing in this diary for over **a week**. It doesn't really feel like that much time has passed. Maybe it's because we've been training so hard at school. By the way, **I received another performance sheet**.

RUNT'S PERFORMANCE:

FARMING	12%
BUILDING	3%
CRAFTING	6%

LEVEL 7

I'm sure it's because the teachers didn't like our furnace house. Again, this is **totally unfair**. My level is still horrible, too. Despite all of my hard training, **I'm only level 7**.

Even **Bumbi's** score is higher than mine. **Bumbi is this really weird kid**. But he's really good at both farming and building things.

My building score is holding my level back. If I want to improve it, I'll have to do extra well in building class. Which means . . . **I have to build stuff the teachers actually like**.

But I still don't see what was so bad about **the furnace house**.

I'm going to have to think about this. There must be a reason why the teachers liked those mushroom houses. **But why?**

Think.

Think.

Think.

I'd be happy with even **level 20 at this point.**
Sigh. I am so pathetic!

Of course, **Max** has been bragging because he's **level 15** now. **How can I catch up to him?** This is a lot harder than I thought!

I've decided to spend **Sunday nights practicing my building.** I've got to raise my score.

Stump and I discussed why the teachers didn't like our **furnace house**.

"Well, they did say the **mushroom houses were beautiful**," Stump said. "Maybe that's the reason?"

"No," I said. "**The teachers are tricky.** They'd never tell us the real reason. They want us to figure that out for ourselves."

"Hurrrrrr."

". . ."

". . ."

We talked the whole morning. Eventually I had an idea.

"Maybe it's about **efficiency**," I said.

"Efficiency?"

"Here's the thing. What does it **take** to make a mushroom house?"

"A mushroom."

"Exactly."

* * *

Here's my idea on why the teachers graded the girls' mushroom houses so highly:

A mushroom house is made out of a giant red mushroom. All it takes to create a giant red mushroom is:

- **One red mushroom**
- **One bone meal**

What that means is, you don't need a lot of materials to make a mushroom house. If you're stranded out in the wilderness and it's starting to rain, **a mushroom house can provide instant shelter**. All you need to do is sprinkle some bone meal onto a red mushroom, and **BAM**, you have the basic shell of a house. Or a roof **at the very least**.

On the other hand, it takes **eight cobblestones** to make a **single furnace**. In other words, making a house out of furnaces is **very, very inefficient**. You can't make such a house unless you have a ton of cobblestone on hand.

I shared this idea with my pal Stump.

"Hurggggg."

Hurggggg? That's the sound a villager makes when he's thinking **real hard**. But then Stump agreed with me.

"**That has to be it**," he said, nodding. "What's funny is, the girls weren't even aware of how great their house was. They just made it because they thought it was **cute**."

"Right."

"Don't worry," said Stump. "Now that we know this, our building scores **are going to take off**."

"I hope so."

"I'm sure of it," he said. "Still . . . " He paused.

I guessed what he was going to say, so I finished his sentence for him. "We have to figure out something **even better than a mushroom house**."

Break's over.
Back to school.

In building class, I **listened intently** to what the teachers said. I **observed** everything.

In two days, there will be another building project.
Stump and I must prepare for that day.

We're going to think of something good to build. Something that **amazes** the teachers. Something that wipes the smirk **off Max's face**. In three days, when I get another performance sheet, it's going to have a good building score.

I glanced at Stump during building class and saw a gleam in his eye. He was thinking the same thing.

Yeah.
We're going to build something absolutely crazy.

Hejjo!!!
My name is Runt!
I am a noobmuffin!!!
The end.

Hurrrrrrg.

That was Max trolling me. He took my diary. I didn't even notice. I was at school, it was lunchtime, and I was about to write in here. Then Max's buddy **Razberry** started asking me a ton of **totally ridiculous** questions about fishing.

"Hey, Runt. Do you like **fishing** more than you like **cows?**"

"Have you ever caught a **squid?**"

"Is it possible to **swim and fish** at the same time?"

Well, I was so confused, I set my diary down and turned to face him. At that point, Razberry paused—he was probably running out of things to ask. I guess three questions is **a lot for him**. Then, he just started asking random stuff, like:

"Have you ever milked a **mooshroom?**"

I just sighed, and turned back to my diary. Little did I know, in the short time that I was listening to **Razberry, Max** had taken my diary and written that stuff in it.

So **Razberry** was just distracting me.

I know what you're thinking. I know.

I'm a **total noob** to fall for such a trick.

But **my mind** has been elsewhere lately. I've been thinking about the upcoming test. Anyway, I shouldn't be wasting time talking about **Razberry** and **Max**.

Moving on.

* * *

The mobs tried something new last night. A few **spiders** carried **zombies** up and over the wall. Then the zombies waited outside until morning, until they caught on **fire from the sun**. Then, while they were burning, the zombies walked up next to the wooden houses and tried to set them on fire. **Our house was one of them.** Mom, Dad, and I were so scared! We could hear the **zombies** laughing as they burned. **It was horrible!** All we could do was pray for a warrior like **Steve** to show up.

He didn't show up.

But it started raining, which put an end to the **burning zombies' devious plan**. The mobs retreated after that. Even so, their attack wasn't a total failure: When I walked to school, the stench of wet zombie hung in the air. It was a **horrible smell**, kind of like **rotten apples mixed with sweaty feet**.

51

I guess I can add **apples** to the list of things I won't be able to stomach for a while. If the mobs ever figure out a way to make **cookies and cake** seem disgusting, I'm going to be in a lot of trouble.

* * *

Before class, assistants handed out a **new type of performance sheet**. I guess the teachers thought it was a waste to keep crafting sheets for all 150 students. So one of the elders came up with a **special type of book** that displays a student's grades automatically. Kind of like how a map updates your position and changes the landscape. Well, this is the report card version of that. They're called **"record books."**

They're pretty tough to make, so, if a student loses his or her record book, the teachers will charge **three emeralds** for a new one.

I'll have to guard mine, since I'm sure Max will tear it up if he gets ahold of it. Or write something like **"noobmuffin"** in it.

Here's my record book. It's got that purple shimmer that most enchanted items have.

Pretty cool, hurrn?

(Besides the bad grades, I mean. A combat score of 2% . . . I really am a noobmuffin. It'd be zero if I hadn't crafted a wooden sword, though. **Thanks, Steve.***)*

RUNT
STUDENT
LEVEL 7

MINING	1%
COMBAT	2%
TRADING	1%
FARMING	12%
BUILDING	3%
CRAFTING	6%

As you can see, a record book includes **additional skills** that the old performance sheets did not: **mining, combat, and trading**. Things are getting more complicated at school already.

It's because of the mobs. The mobs keep attacking almost every night, in greater and greater numbers. Even the village elders, **wimpy** as they are, well . . . even they know we have to start fighting back.

Some day, those mobs are going to **pay**.
And I plan to be there when that happens.

* * *

I **daydreamed** through the first class this morning, Crafting Basics. I couldn't stop thinking about the upcoming building **test**. The best way for me to raise my student level is by improving my **building score** since apparently <u>building is my weakness</u>.

I mean, I was so sure a **furnace house** was **awesome** and **amazing**, but according to the teachers, my **building ideas** are about as good as a **zombie pigman's**. No. Not even that good. More like a **slime's** . . .

That was why I paid a lot more attention in today's second class: **Essential Wall Building**. The teacher showed us a short comic about obsidian. **Mining a single block of obsidian** takes forever, and if you stop mining a block before you are done, the block will revert back to its un-mined state, and you'll have to start all over again.

The comic illustrated the problems miners face digging for obsidian. Mining obsidian doesn't take **that long**. It's just an exaggeration. But from what I've heard, it can **feel like forever**.

The head teacher burst into the classroom and told us:

"School's out early today. Class is over!!!"

Well, after hearing such good news, I leapt up from my desk so high, it was as if I'd chugged down a <u>Potion of Leaping II</u>.

No class! That meant **Stump** and I could practice the rest of the day for our **building test**. We could go over all of our building **ideas** again. We could sit in the grass at the edge of the village, chat, and watch the **rectangular clouds drift by**, like we used to do when we were little. **I was really excited!**

Then the head teacher told us why school was being let out early.

It was for our own **safety**.
Something had happened
in the village while we were in class.

Something involving an outsider. The head teacher called it the "**outsider incident.**" One thing I know for certain is when an adult uses that word—**incident**—you know something bad has happened.

Once, there was a "pumpkin incident," when Stump and I ran around the village with pumpkins on our heads. We also stuck our arms out like zombies and made weird noises. We were trying to sound like **endermen**, but we didn't know what an enderman sounded like back then. Looking back, the sounds we made were more like the **clucks of a chicken crossed with a cow's mooing.**

Some old man thought we were a kind of **new monster.** When he saw us, he screamed and ran off to tell the elders. **The whole village was in a panic.** As you can imagine, Stump and I got into a **LOT of trouble.**

It's great to know that today's incident had nothing to do with me. My dad told me the whole story when I got home. He witnessed most of it, I guess. You see, this morning, **an outsider came into the village.** Someone we'd never met before. He looked a little bit like Steve, but **he said his name was Mike.**

* * *

Apparently, Mike **wasn't a happy kind of person.**
Not like Steve.

Or that **wolf guy** who sometimes visits us—I forget his name. Anyway, even though Mike seemed so angry, it didn't stop villagers from trying to trade with him. After all, he had a few emeralds. **Hey, we villagers don't discriminate, as long as there's a glint of the green stuff.**

Here's where the problems started. Every time Mike tried trading with a villager, he got even angrier. Didn't like all the sounds the villagers were making. Kept complaining about it—said the villagers around him sounded like a bunch of **giraffes** that drank way too much coffee.

Honestly, I don't know what a **giraffe** is, or **coffee**. But I'd really like to know. Many of the villagers near Mike were just as curious. Their **"hurrrrrs"** and **"rhurrrrgs"** and **"hurrrrns"** grew louder.

This, in turn, **annoyed Mike** even more. To make fun of them, he started **mimicking** the sounds the villagers made. And he kept calling them "giraffes." This caused the villagers to make **even more noise**. They were so curious about these new words. A few villagers even wanted to trade for these things **without even knowing** what they were.

"Giraffe?" said a villager. "Is that like a **mooshroom**? How many you got? And how much for one?"

Then a girl walked up to him and said, "What is **coffee? Hurrrrrrn?** I want to try some!"

"Me too!" shouted another.

A man pushed through the crowd. "I'll trade **five emeralds** for some coffee!"

"Six emeralds!" bellowed an old man.

Another old man: **"Ten! Ten emeralds!"**

Even an **iron golem** approached, and in a deep, awkward voice said: **"Me-also-want-coffee."**

Finally, Mike just **shouted** at them all. Said something about how he didn't want to trade anyway, because **no one had enchanted stuff**. He ran off as the villagers chased him: the words "giraffe" and "coffee" were spoken at least a thousand times. Somehow, Mike lost them in the streets.

Then he ran into **Bub**.

Bub's a farmer. <u>A really nice one.</u> Quiet. Helpful. What's more, Bub never tries to cheat anyone in a trade. He'll give you a good deal every time. Also, he had a really nice enchanted iron **pickaxe** he'd been **wanting to sell**. In other words, Bub was just the kind of villager Mike was looking for. Mike and Bub started talking outside of Bub's farm. Just as the crowd of villagers spotted him again, Mike and Bub stepped into Bub's house. That was the **last time** anyone saw either of them. Several villagers waited outside for Mike to return, so they could pester him about giraffes again. Yet, **Mike never came back out**. At some point, the villagers got tired of waiting around and opened the door to Bub's house. **No one was there.**

Both of them
were gone!!!

Obviously, **Mike had done something**. But what? Where had they gone?

Of course, we've had problems with outsiders before.

- **Noobs stealing our vegetables** (such as that guy from last week).
- **Noobs stealing from blacksmith chests.**
- Actually, **noobs stealing anything that can possibly be stolen.** Even wool blocks from our street lamps.
- **Griefers setting fire to our crops.**
- **Weird guys trying to pass off big green seeds as emeralds in trades.** (Seriously. How stupid do outsiders think we are?)
- **Warriors using our furnaces.**

Once, my family couldn't even cook dinner because this warrior charged into our house and began using our furnace to smelt a stack of iron ore. He didn't even ask or say hello—just **boom**, walked in, and started smelting in front of us . . . **without saying a single word.**

My dad, being the **real nice guy** that he is, didn't yell at the intruder. He simply crafted **another furnace** for us to cook food with.

Maybe you can guess what the warrior did.

Yeah, he just said, "**Thanks,**" then used that second furnace to smelt another stack of ore.

Hurrrrrg.

But then, all of that **isn't so bad**, compared to this. **An abduction?** In our village? **What's going on?**

It's the first time a villager has ever been kidnapped before. Why would someone want to **kidnap Bub**, anyway? What's the point?

It's really **kind of strange**. Thankfully, we're pretty sure Bub wasn't hurt. If he had been, at least one of our iron golems would have **gone crazy**. Yet, not one of them did anything this morning. Well, except hand out **flowers** as usual. While I was gazing out of my bedroom window, I saw an iron golem trying to give away a **flower**. I guess it didn't know what to do, because there weren't any kids outside, due to the "Mike incident."

I just hope they can **find Bub**. We kids can't go outside until they do. Until the elders say it's **safe** again.

Oi.

How boring.

That means there's **no school tomorrow** as well. So the building test is postponed. Maybe we'll have it Friday, who knows.

Oi, oi, oi.

Whatever. It gives me more time to prepare. Even if I can't see **Stump** today or tomorrow, I can think of some stuff to build. I'm sure Stump's doing the same right now. Also, I'll get some **building practice in**.

Okay, I'm off . . .
See ya, diary!

WEDNESDAY

First, some **good news**.

I **built** some walls in my bedroom last night. Every time I built one, I **destroyed** it, then **built another** out of a different material. My mom wasn't too **happy** about that. I was making a lot of noise, and because of the walls, she couldn't even open the door to find out what was going on.

The things we students do to get better, **hurrrr**?

After all that grueling work, though, my building score **went up.**

RUNT
STUDENT
LEVEL 7

MINING	1%
COMBAT	2%
TRADING	1%
FARMING	12%
BUILDING	5%
CRAFTING	6%

63

It didn't go up by much—from 3 to 5%—but it's better than nothing, right?

Strangely, this means:

1) the record book can somehow judge my progress and
2) update on its own. It's a pretty cool item the elders came up with.

How did they craft it, I wonder? The elders might be wimpy old men, but they're pretty clever. They can create things that even warriors can't. Secret things. Our knowledge goes way back.

Now, don't go thinking I can just sit in my room all day, build some walls, and raise my building score to 100%.

I think the only reason I was able to do that was because of my horribly low score. I'll try again tonight and see what happens.

As for the bad news?

No, there's no bad news today.

The mobs didn't attack at all last night. Maybe Tuesday night is their night off? I wonder what the mobs do to relax.

* * *

A little update. Somehow, it's only good news today. Some woman found Bub. She's a friend of his. She was walking by his house and heard faint shouting. It was coming from the ground under Bub's house.

It didn't take very long for the miners to find him. They tore apart the whole floor of Bub's house.

It turned out he had been sealed **underground**, in cobblestone.

Don't worry, **he's alive**. His house, though . . . it's seen **better** days. To look at it, you'd think a family of creepers went off underneath it.

Now, one might be wondering why Bub was trapped in cobblestone **under his house**. Why would Mike do something like that? What did he have to gain?

We have a general idea. Mike trapped Bub there because he **didn't have enough** emeralds for Bub's pickaxe. Whenever Mike found enough, he could come back to trade. He was "**saving**" Bub, then. He was smart enough to not attack the farmer, since our **iron golems** would clobber him in response.

It's **kind of sad**. Sometimes, the outsiders treat us worse than the mobs do. Some only think of us villagers as walking **trading machines**. "**Hey, this guy's trading some good stuff. Better seal him up in stone.**"

It's not right, **you know**? We're people, too.

Honestly, there's only one reason the elders still let us talk to outsiders. **Steve**.

Actually, in some strange way, the "**incident**" **actually helped**. It made us **feel better** about ourselves . . . because we took care of it without the help of Steve. Steve's great and all, but <u>we can't always rely on him to save the day, now can we?</u>

As for Mike, he'd better not come back. That's all I have to say. Stump tricked an iron golem into thinking that Mike is a new kind of **zombie**. It was the same iron golem that wanted coffee yesterday. So he told the golem that Mike is a coffee zombie.

If the golem smashes Mike, it will find **coffee instead of a zombie's usual rotten flesh**.

That set the golem off. It's been walking around the village all day, in search mode, its eyes glowing brightly.

Stump is **pretty cool**. That's why he's my **best friend** and **building partner**. I can always count on him to come up with cool stuff, too.

We're still not sure why that golem wants coffee, though. Maybe because all those villagers wanted it? Maybe if the golem ever **found** some coffee, it'd start handing it out to the adults, the same way they give flowers to kids? **Mhm . . .**

* * *

After the village settled down, Stump and I spent the rest of the day at our old hangout spot. **The old field next to the wall**. He brought a **cake** from his house (his parents are bakers, remember—that's why his family is good at crafting). And yes, while we powered through slice after slice of the **best cake in Minecraftia, we came up with a pretty good building idea.**

I'm not going to write about it in here, though. Not yet. It's **top secret**, you know? If Max stole my diary again and read this section, he'd know all about **Project X**.

I'm warning you now, though. Don't get your hopes up. It's not the **most interesting** house. But hey, it's sure to win the teachers' hearts. That's what matters right now. I'm thinking my **building score will reach 10%** after this.

Hurrrrr. I'm getting all excited about a building score of 10%.
How pathetic am I?

* * *

Some time later, as we sat in the grass and gazed at the clouds, we found a book:

The Adventures of Cow the Cow—Volume 115

Someone had stashed it in the tall grass. Max must come to this spot to read. I flipped through a few pages, and had to put it down. **Grammar, spelling** . . . Cow the Cow didn't need such things. Nor did he need an actual story. The book was pretty much just him walking around randomly, talking to mobs.

I won't even comment on the artwork.

So the **president of Minecraftia** is a huge fan of the cow, eh? **Yeah. I highly doubt it.**

In fact, I don't think Minecraftia even has **a president**. I think that's only a fake review for that silly book.

What a scam.

I really don't get it. Max wants to be a librarian, so why is he **reading this stuff?** It really makes **no sense**, you know? At least now I know where he got **"hejjo"** from . . .

Come to think of it, I haven't seen Max much recently. That's the final **good news** of today! No, there's even more **good news: we have**

school tomorrow. It's really **weird**, but I'm actually **happy** about it. Well, the building test isn't until **Friday**. I recently found that out, but that's okay. It gives Stump and me even more time to work on **Project X.** That's what we're calling our house idea. It makes it sound **cool** and **mysterious**, you know? I mean, let's say you're out getting ice cream with a friend, and there are all these kids around. You could mention your **"school project,"** and get **totally beat up**. Or, you could say something about **"Project X."** Just slip it into your conversation, real casual:

"**Project X** is coming along pretty good."

"Yeah, we'll be in the final stages **soon**."

"Just a few **more** experiments."

"Yes. **Just a few more**."

By the way, the **ice cream in our village rocks**. I think I'll go get some Friday after the building test. We've got all the flavors.

Creeper crunch.

Ghast tear swirl.

Magma cream ripple.

My favorite is **diamond ore chunk.**

YUMM!!!

Something **super lame** happened this morning.

It all started **a few weeks** ago, when my mom's best friend said she saw a **creeper in the village**. During the day. She didn't see much of it, she said. Only its face. It was hiding in some tall grass near a wheat crop. The past few days, more and more of my mom's friends keep saying they've seen this creeper. By all accounts, you'll only see it out of the **corner of your eye**. Or, maybe you'll see it pop up out of some hiding spot. But only for a split second, and always just its sad little face. Then **poof**—it's gone.

The village creeper
exhibit #1

Pretty hard to believe, honestly. Last week, when I told Steve about it, he said it reminded him of **UFO** or **Bigfoot** sightings. Whatever those are. He said it could be the result of **people's imaginations**. After all, why would a creeper sneak around a village? **It makes no sense!!!**

I had to agree. Sadly, my mom's not as skeptical. So after I woke up this morning, she handed me **a leash** . . . and pointed at Fluffles.

Yeah. Fluffles is our cat. I had to bring him with me to school today. As you probably know, **creepers are terrified of cats.** My mom just wanted me to be safe. It wouldn't have been so bad if Fluffles  had been a **fully-grown ocelot**, but he's just a **baby**. No one else had to bring a cat to school during this **"creeper scare,"** of course. As you can imagine, Max took **full advantage** of this. He made kitten noises whenever he passed me in the hall. Later, he pretended to be afraid of Fluffles; started calling him **"Danger Kitty."**

There was nothing I could say, really. (Hey, I didn't need to say anything. I'll get my **revenge**. After Stump and I unveil **Project X**, Max is going to cry like a **baby ghast**.)

Fluffles kept meowing during class, too. More than a few teachers glared at me. I'll admit, at one point, I even thought about **shoving Fluffles** into my school chest (Steve says they're called **"lockers"** in his world). Knowing me, though, I'd forget all about him and **leave him at school, then I'd get grounded for months**. Probably my mom would come to school and tell my teachers (in front of every student) to please **make sure** I took Fluffles home.

Whatever. It doesn't matter. Max already knows the kitten's name. He made sure to rub it in whenever he could with stuff like:

"Hey there, **Warrior Runt!** How's Fluffles?"

And later: "Warrior Runt! Sir! I hate to interrupt you, **my lord!** Please forgive me! I just want to know. How **many creepers** did **Grandmaster Fluffles** slay today?"

This is the part where I'd write **"hurrrrg"** a bunch. I won't, though. After today, **I don't have the energy to be angry.** I'm just going to go back to our hangout spot and work on the house.

Tomorrow is the test. Finally **!!/**

If I fail tomorrow, my chances of **becoming a warrior** are pretty much done with.

And I'm **having doubts** about my house idea. Maybe it's not **good** at all. Maybe the teachers will **hate it**, just like they hated my **furnace house.**

What would a warrior do?

Better yet, **what would Steve do?** I've been wanting to get his opinion on my **house idea**, but he hasn't been around lately.

It's **just me**, now.
Tomorrow, **all I can do is try.**

The mobs **creeper bombed** us again last night. I woke up to the sound of **baby slimes** raining down upon the roof of our house.

All the slimes **were gone** by sunrise, though. How they managed to leave the city, with the wall being there, **I don't know. And I don't care**. I'm not complaining at all. It meant me being able to walk to school without "incident."

"Incident." Thinking about slimes and that word at the same time makes me remember the **"slime incident."** That's something I've been trying to forget. Once, **when I was ten years old**, I was **attacked** by a baby slime. The thing had been waiting in a dark alley all night. Waiting for a **kid** like me to just come strolling by. When it jumped out at me, **I panicked**, and **ended up drop kicking** the thing as hard as I could. It went flying through a window into some woman's house. Somehow, it landed in the furnace—she'd left coal in the fuel tray, and the slime started **cooking**. Baking, rather.

She thought I'd done **it intentionally**, and again, the **elders were involved, and my parents**. It took hours of explaining just to clear my name. By then, the woman's house reeked of what could only be described as **slime casserole**.

After I arrived at school, though, I forgot all about slimes.

Every student was nervous today. Except **Max** and **Razberry**. All 150 students were just standing around at the edge of the village. In a flat field perfect for building tons of houses.

Each student had a building partner, which meant there were seventy-five teams. Sara teamed up with Ariel again. I guessed they were probably going to make another mushroom house. Maybe some improved variant. Each team was given a section of the field to build in. Wooden signs were placed in each team's designated area. Stump and I make up the team known as . . . **"Danger Kitty."** I chose that name to spite Max. My thoughts were, after we beat him, the teachers would call out our team name and he'd be furious. Of course, Max is a good builder. I can't deny that. Even if we do beat him, it'll only be by a few points. **Urrrrg,** the test will begin shortly. I'll update soon . . .

* * *

<u>Well.</u>

We finished our house.

Here it is. **Don't laugh**, please. We think **efficiency** is what the teachers want, remember?

And now, it's time to unveil . . .

PROJECT X

LIKE A BOSS.

The overall idea is a bit similar to the old furnace house—except with fewer furnaces and less space, and with additional things such as a crafting table, an enchanting table, and even farms.

To save space, the bed is built into the roof.

To cut down on block usage, part of the roof is made of stone slabs. You can craft two stone slabs with one block of cobblestone.

The inside is pretty compact.

We turned two squares of dirt floor into a wheat farm.

There's an enchanting table, and one wall is a bookcase to power up the table slightly. A crafting table and multiple furnaces are all accessible. Due to lack of space, a torch had to be set onto one furnace.

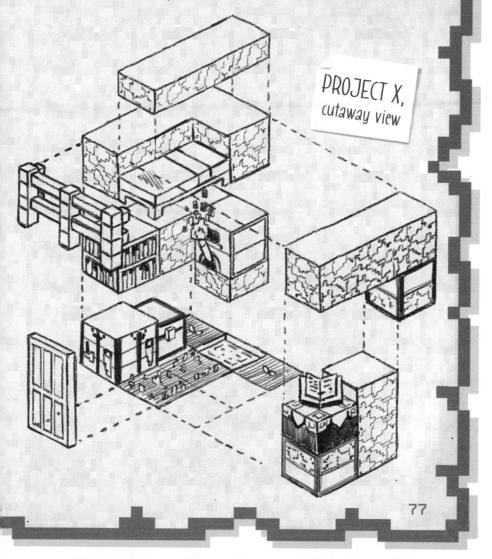

PROJECT X,
cutaway view

(By the way, the enchanting table was given to us. We obviously can't craft such a thing. Its inclusion also won't raise our score. It's just to show what's possible.)

Oh, about the chest on the left. The lid wouldn't open with a wall above it. We used some upside-down stairs there.

Note the two patches of farmland on the corners. One area is for melons. The other, for pumpkins. They're both accessible from the inside. You just have to reach your arms across some blocks.

Our whole idea was to make a house that offered as much as possible, while taking as little as possible to construct.

EFFICIENCY,
in other words.

To come up with this idea, Stump and I imagined ourselves as warriors. If we were far away from the village, we wouldn't have tons of materials to build with. We'd have to be efficient.

So we thought and thought,
and ended up with this.
It's the ultimate survival house.

I mean, let's say creepers blew up the whole world—every block in **Minecraftia**, gone, except for this house. No problem. We could still survive forever in this house. It'd be boring, though. It'd be a life of standing in a tiny little house, eating nothing but bread. Sometimes a pumpkin. Drinking water. **That's all.**

That was another reason why we included a bookcase. During such an end-of-the-world scenario, at least you'd have something to read. But while we were building the house today, Stump and I ran into a problem. One of the books in the bookcase was . . . super lame. Lamer than any of Max's favorite books. *Diary of a Grass Block.*

I honestly don't know how it got there. And I was really hoping the teachers wouldn't spot it.

I mean, the book's description is something like:

Have you ever wondered what it would be like to be a grass

block? What problems does a grass block face during grass block

school? What does a grass block eat? What does a grass block do

for fun? Come find out in this diary of a grass block written by

an eleven-year-old grass block!

Number of pages: 7

Wow.
Just wow.

The teachers would fail us for sure if they saw that. Whenever a teacher got close to the bookshelf, I made sure to stand in front of it, particularly that book.

Anyway, I don't know if the teachers will like Project X . . . **After all, Max's house is kind of cool as well:**

Team
Creeper Biscuit

He and Razberry took the girl's **mushroom house idea** from that last building test, and dumped lava all over it. That's how they discovered that lava doesn't burn giant mushrooms.

Not only does the **lava**:

1) prevent mobs from attacking,

2) it lights up the area.

You could find such a house pretty easily at night.

I hate to admit it,

but it's not a bad idea.

However, many others didn't have such **great houses**.
Such as the kids next to us. **They built a dirt house.**

TEAM
NOOBMUFFIN

By the way, **"Team Noobmuffin"** isn't their real team name. Max replaced their sign with one of his own.

* * *

After our building time was up, everyone just waited for the outcome.

The teachers were **"hurgg"ing** a lot.

Students' faces were **grim**.

Not too many were talking.

I was kind of afraid.

No, not "kind of." The fear I felt was heavy as a furnace in my stomach. No, worse than that. It was the same as when I ate a slice of that cake Sara crafted a couple months ago.

That cake was **so hard, I remember**. It probably could have been used as a weapon of some kind. But I didn't want to hurt her feelings, so I ate it. To accomplish this, I had to dunk my cake slice into a bucket of **milk** just to get it soft enough to chew.

Sorry, I'm rambling.
I do that when I'm **nervous**.

* * *

<u>**Update:**</u> Now, the teachers are gathering . . . They're going to announce the **top three** house designs. Stump's sitting next to me, eyes wide and filled with fear. He wants to be a **warrior**, too.

This is it!!!
It's all or nothing.
We're just waiting.
Waiting.
Waiting.
And then . . .

* * *

Update:
HURGGGGGGGGGGGGGGGGGGGGGGGGGGGGGGG.
HURGGGGGGGGGGGGGGGG.
Hurggggggg.
Hurgurrgurgurgurgrugrgrurgurgggggggggggggg.

. . .

. . .

. . .

Hurgg.

(Sorry.)

I just had to get that out.

I'm . . . going crazy.

Let me explain. Standing before **150 silent students**, the head teacher said: **"In first place** for best house design is . . .

Team Danger Kitty."
I honestly couldn't believe it.

The teachers praised our house even more than the girls' mushroom house from before. **It was a miracle.**

The most efficient house they've ever seen.

Their words.

Not a daydream. Not my **imagination**.

I couldn't help but smile when Max freaked out. For a second, I almost felt sorry for him, until I remembered all the harassment he had given me the other day.

Even now, I'm so **stunned**, I can barely even write. So forgive me if I don't write much right now . . . I'll update later when my heart stops pounding and my hands stop shaking.

✳ ✳ ✳

Okay, so the teachers said our house still has some flaws. Like, a few things could have been done better. Still, they used the word "impressive."

Impressive.

Actually, another word came before that one—"very."

Very impressive.

(I'm not going to "hurgg" again. I promise. **I'll keep it under control.**)

I gave Stump a **huge high five**. He was responsible for half of the design. A lot of students came up and **congratulated** us afterward. **Not Max,** though.

"Too bad warriors aren't all about building," was all he said.

His buddy Razberry chimed in: "**Yeah.** You can't build mobs to death. **Nooblords.**"

I don't care about what he said, though.

It's the first real **accomplishment** I've ever had in my life.

I'm too happy right now.

At one point, Stump nudged me with his elbow.

"Runt," he said. **"Our. Scores. Look."**

He was so **excited**, he couldn't even speak in sentences, just single words. I was still out of it myself. The shock of such a huge success was still flooding my mind. **I eventually realized** my friend was staring at his record book. When I saw his building score, **I couldn't even breathe.** It was insanely high.

STUMP
STUDENT
LEVEL 16

MINING	1%
COMBAT	0%
TRADING	5%
FARMING	7%
BUILDING	61%
CRAFTING	23%

And now, he was level 16.

He was level 3 yesterday. He went from 3 to 16. BOOM!!!
Just like that.

I whipped out my own record book and stared at it in **total disbelief.** Farming, crafting, and building all went up from our efforts. Obviously, the biggest gain was in building.

A jump of 60%.

```
      RUNT
      STUDENT
   LEVEL 17

  MINING              1%
  COMBAT              2%
  TRADING             1%
  FARMING            25%
  BUILDING           65%
  CRAFTING            9%
```

I tried to sneak a peek at **Max's record book**, but he wouldn't let me. He was being as **secretive** with his record book as he is with those ridiculous cow books.

Last time I saw, he was **level 15**. Maybe he's **level 20**, now? I'm catching up, then. If I keep doing well, and working this hard, I might **overtake** him. His team got **third place in the competition**, though, so I probably didn't make huge gains on him. The only thing holding his design back was the inherent **danger** that came from **walls of lava**.

A different team of girls got **second place**. They had a similar idea to ours. Their house was **basically** just a **hole in the ground**, set up with crafting tables and such.

* * *

Even though it's Friday, there was no **Mob Defense** class. They let us off the hook. They said we had to do some <u>reading</u> about mobs **on our own** this weekend.

At the end of the day, **I got ice cream** with Stump, Sara, and Ariel. Their team got **eleventh place,** which is still respectable. Sara says they're going to **work harder** for the next building test.

While we ate our ice cream, the four of us decided to **form a partnership.** We'll share our building ideas, and attempt to **shut Max out** of the next test. Those girls aren't exactly **friends** with him, either. However, there're going to be many more tests, and not all of them are going to deal with building. From farming to mining, we'll cover everything.

For now, I just need to **relax a bit**.

I've been **stressing** myself out.

Hurrrrmmmmmmmmm.

This diamond ore chunk is **amazing**.

Today, my dad made me go **fishing** with him.

After yesterday, I must have used up **all of my luck**, because I only snagged junk. Sticks, sticks, and more sticks. And bowls, and a leather boot. **Even another fishing rod.**

Probably someone had had just as much luck as I was having, tossed the rod in, and called it a day. That was what I felt like doing after **I reeled in a bone.**

Beyond that, **today was uneventful.** I didn't do anything else. Didn't practice. Didn't talk to anyone about any **projects or ideas**. Didn't even see Stump, as his parents were making him help out with baking a **big cake** for the mayor.

My parents didn't really say much about my building **achievement**. They're farmers. They figure I'll become a farmer just like them.

I've never told them about my dreams.

I'm not sure what my dad's reaction will be if he ever finds out. But now, **I'm exhausted**. Worrying about the future is for another day.

* * *

As the square sun sank into the blocky horizon, I curled up on my bed with my favorite history book. It was written by some old villager from a distant land. Sounds boring, right?

Well, this is **Minecraftia**. In this world, even history can be pretty entertaining. Besides, the guy who wrote it was a warrior villager. The only one in history.

After he took up the sword, his village exiled him forever, and he wandered the land **like Steve**.

I flipped to the chapter on legendary mobs. Some were downright scary, such as **Mungo the Overlord**.

According to legend, **Mungo is the freakiest zombie pigman** that ever lived. He's as tall as any enderman, and wields two enchanted gold swords. One in each hand.

Mungo is so big, his swords look like little toys in his huge, meaty mitts.

Long ago, before I was born, he **destroyed a village** almost as big as ours. I know, it sounds like something Max would make up, right? But it's all right here in this book. We villagers never go into the Nether, and tonight, **I'm super thankful for that.**

Once per year, he leaves the Nether and roams through the Overworld, hunting for noobs and warriors **alike.** He's so big, he can **swallow a creeper whole**, and he's so strong, he'll survive the explosion—the worst damage being a bad case of gas. The history book literally describes Mungo's huge farts after he eats a creeper. *(No, my friends, don't ever stand downwind of Mungo after he's devoured a charged creeper. It won't be a pleasant experience.)*

While reading that history book, I couldn't help but **think** about Steve.

It seems like **forever** since I last saw him.

What happened to him?

I hope he comes back soon.

This morning, **we had visitors.** They weren't outsiders, though. They were other **villagers**. A lot of them, too, at least **twenty**. It caused a huge buzz in Villagetown. Other villagers have visited us before, but never at a time like this, what with all the mob attacks recently.

The elders told us that they're **just tourists**, traveling around.

I'm not so sure.

I mean, if they were just traveling about **Minecraftia**,

they'd look a **little happy**, right?

Smile.

Wave.

Greet us.

Right?

Not them.

They were obviously **sad**. They just stared at the ground, their faces **gloomy**. And the elders ushered them all into the village hall. Hours later, our builders made them a **brand new house**. A house big enough to hold all twenty of them.

The "tourists" only seemed to get sadder at this. I don't know what's going on with them, but Stump and I think they're not tourists at all. But our mayor **assured** us that they're really just travelers. There's nothing to worry about, he said. Things are **totally fine,** he said. Everything is **absolutely, positively cool and okay.** He said that last sentence with a huge grin and two thumbs up—while standing in front of these people:

No, there's **nothing sad about them at all!**

See, the father on the left, he's just stunned at how awesome our village is. His daughter? Well, those are **tears of happiness,** nothing more. As for the mom, she's only worried because she forgot to feed the dog before they left.

Totally.

At least, something like that is what the mayor wants us to believe . . .

Noooo, something weird is going on. I tried talking to that crying girl today, but the elders won't let anyone go near that newly built house. **Mmmmh, It's really quite mysterious.**

93

Of course, I asked the guards at the door why I couldn't go in and say hello to our new guests. **They're tourists, right?** I should welcome them, right?

But the guards said, "They're exhausted from traveling. They need to rest. **Please come back later, Runt.**"

Hmmmmm. I will get to the bottom of this. **Detective Runt is on the job.**

School was fairly **standard** today. Let me skip past all that **and just say** . . .

Steve came back.

I ran into him after school. He was walking down the street. **Slowly.** And the **look** on his face . . . I'd never seen him like that before.

"Steve!" I shouted, running up to him. "What happened to you?"

He coughed, shook his head. "I . . . **need some water**," he said.

His voice was raspy. He looked tired. Beat up. As if he'd **fought Mungo the Overlord** for days and finally emerged victorious.

"Follow me," I said, and led him back to my house.

I gave him a bucket of milk and two loaves of bread—fresh out of the furnace. He chugged down the whole bucket, **glug, glug, glug**, then wolfed down each loaf in a few bites. It seemed like he hadn't had any food or water in days. After, he rested his back against the wall of the living room, closed his eyes, and slid down against the wall.

"Steve," I said. **"Answer me, hurrr? What's going on?"**

"My base," he said. "It's **gone**."

What? From what I understood, his "base" was his main house, a really nice one. He had a lot of houses scattered out there, in the wilderness, but his base was the **best one**.

"What do you mean, gone?"

"Just **gone**," he said. "Everything I had is all gone. My base, gone. My houses, gone. My diamond tools, enchanted armor, and rail system. **All gone.**"

"How? Who did this?"

And suddenly, I thought I knew the answer. **I figured it was Mike.** He's like the **evil version** of Steve. But what Steve said next really surprised me.

"The mobs," he said. "They came in the night. **Zombies digging through dirt. Creepers exploding. Endermen tearing apart cobblestone.** They destroyed everything I had."

He paused.

"**I died again, Runt.** I died several times in fact. And every time I died, I kept going back. Kept trying to retrieve my items. Kept trying to save my house . . ."

I said nothing, only waited for him to continue. My thoughts raced, however. How could the mobs get Steve? **He said his base was indestructible.**

"I've never seen the mobs **act like that before**," he said. "Finally I ran. Ran as fast as I could."

Hurggg.

This is bad.

"I'm homeless now," Steve said. "**I can't believe this.** I don't have anywhere to sleep. I don't even have any food."

"No matter what," I said, "you'll always have a home here. My parents will let you stay with us. I'm sure of it. **Don't worry, okay?**"

"Really? I won't stay long. Just let me get some items again." He sighed. "This means I'll have to punch trees with my bare hands, craft a wooden sword . . . **I'm a noob all over again.**"

"Here," I said. "**Take my wooden sword.** You helped me craft it anyway, remember?"

"All right." Steve stood back up, grabbed my sword with one hand, and wiped sweat from his face with the other.

"I'll be back. I've got to go **speak to your mayor.**"

After he took off, I glanced out at the field, at my parents. They were working the soil, as always. What was the best way to tell them about Steve? They might not like the idea of an outsider staying in our house. **But it's Steve.** How could they say no?

Moments later, I heard a distant scream.

I ran into the streets to **see what was happening.** Another outsider was running through the streets. **He looked terrified.** I'd never seen him before, but I knew who it was—**Mike.**

"**Hey, kid!**" he said, approaching. "**Listen,** I'm sorry about what I did to that farmer guy, but listen! Something crazy is happening!"

"Let me guess," I said. "The mobs destroyed your house."

He gave me a strange look. For some reason, he calmed down a bit.

Mike

"Well, yeah. Anyway, can I stay here? I don't want to go back out there."
I returned his weird look.

"Hurrrn, do I look like the mayor to you?"

"Right. Um, can you take me to him? I'll go to jail. I'll do whatever you guys want. Wash dishes. Milk cows. Whatever. Just don't send me back out there. Last night, I was attacked by about a **hundred** zombies."

And here I thought it was going to be an **easy week**. A week of relaxing, eating ice cream, and taunting Max with my building score.

If the mobs really are becoming as hostile as Steve and Mike claim, our villagers might have to become warriors sooner than the elders think.

I nodded at the outsider in the red shirt.

I shouldn't be nice to him, after what he did to Bub.

Whatever.

I'll let the mayor **decide**.

Besides, from the looks of it, **he's a warrior just like Steve.**
I think we're going to need **all the help we can get**.

I've been so **busy** these days. The classes are becoming more **difficult.** And the homework. **Oh, the homework.**

I'm only writing this entry because I'm taking **a break** from my homework. I really needed one. You see, I did something **really silly** just now.

I set up a crafting table in my bedroom. I had to. My crafting teacher keeps giving us tons of extra assignments that we have to do **at home.**

Craft some **planks.**

Craft some **sticks.**

Craft some **tools.**

Craft, craft, craft. Again, and **again.** And again.

Well, I did that today, after school. I crafted. Oh, did I craft. I surely crafted more than any twelve-year-old villager kid has ever crafted before. But after two hours of crafting, well, I kinda turned into . . . a **zombie.**

A crafting **zombie.** That was totally me.
I just **spaced out.**

I was on my way to crafting **a carpet**, right? I had some wool piled up on the floor next to the table, right? Just slap three wools onto that crafting table and I'd have a shiny new carpet. Right?

Then **Fluffles** came into my room and started sniffing the wool.

Well, I was so tired, I mistakenly picked up **Fluffles** and set him onto the crafting table. I mean, he was the same color (mostly) and the same general shape . . .

Yeah. I tried crafting a carpet with two pieces of wool . . . and a kitten. Needless to say, **that didn't work so well.** I'm pretty sure kittens aren't part of any crafting recipe.

Still, for a moment there, I just couldn't understand why I wasn't able to craft that carpet.

I tried moving the "pieces" around to no avail. Then one of the pieces of "wool" started **meowing**. As I said, I was just too tired.

When you accidentally mistake a kitten for a chunk of wool while trying to craft a carpet, well . . . that's when you know you need to take a break.

Okay.

Break time's over.
I'll write more tomorrow.

You're probably wondering what's going on with **Steve and Mike**.

I'll start with Steve. He's homeless. He was out there, in the wilderness, living on his own. He had a couple houses, I guess, and then **a huge base.**

Well, the mobs destroyed all of them. I still can't believe it, honestly.

Steve's base was pretty incredible. It was a small castle. A small castle made of cobblestone. **Oh, and it had a moat.**

Of lava.

Even so, the mobs **got through.** You're probably wondering how exactly mobs crossed a lava moat. I was wondering the exact same thing.

So I **asked Steve**—and what he told me was pretty hard to believe. Looks like the mobs came up with a new trick. We're calling it the **"witch bridge."**

Here is a **detailed diagram** of the witch bridge. I figure, after I become a famous warrior, I'll have a whole book with such drawings. An encyclopedia of mob tactics.

By the way, what I'm about to show you is top secret.

That means, don't show this to anyone . . .

unless you **absolutely trust them.**

Steve's Base

fire resistance potion

Witch

GLUG
GLUG
GLUG

Here's a side view of Steve's base and lava moat.

As you can see, the lava was two blocks deep and six blocks wide. *(Note the witch on the other side, chugging that fire resistance potion.)*

Now, no mob should have been able to cross that moat. Send in a **million zombies** and they'd all just melt away with nothing to show for it. But those mobs, they're so tricky. They figured out a way.

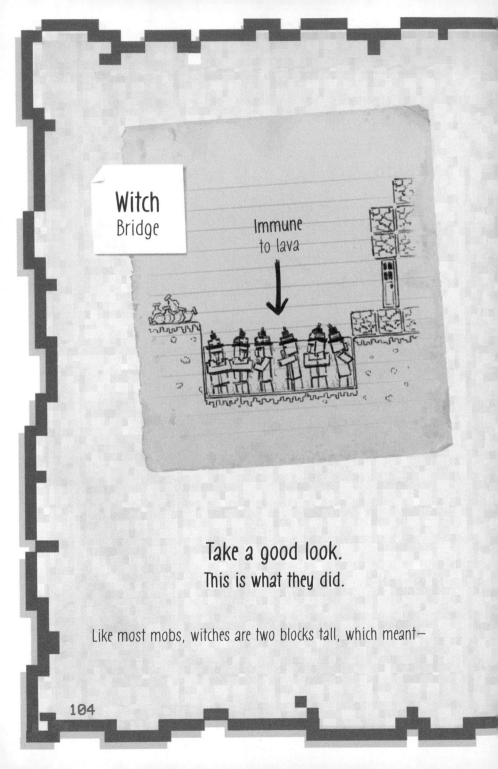

Take a good look.
This is what they did.

Like most mobs, witches are two blocks tall, which meant—

The witches actually made a "bridge" using their own bodies. Their **fire resistance potions** made them immune to lava. So they could swim around in the stuff as if it were water. I guess their potions were of the **upgraded** type.

From what little I understand, upgraded fire resistance potions have a duration of **eight minutes**. I learned that in Brewing Basics (a new class).

In summary, Steve's base was **history.**

Steve actually had to **run from the mobs.**
Him! **A warrior!**
One of the **best!**

I told you the mobs in these parts are nuts. For those of you who don't believe me, well, just come on down. Build a little house. A castle, if you want. Let's see **how long** you last . . .

* * *

Steve talked to the elders and told them what happened. Told them the mobs are getting **feisty.** By the way, that was the word he actually used. **Feisty.**

But then, our village has been dealing with feisty mobs for a while now. It wasn't anything new. The other day, I had to scrape dried slime off our roof. Anyway, the elders said Steve could stay in our village for as **long as he wants.**

However, they can't build him a house. The builders used up a lot of supplies to build that big house for the other villagers.

"The tourists."

So Steve has to build **his own house.** Until he does, he's **staying at my house.** My father built him a bed. He's sleeping in my room.

I guess now would be a good time to give you a **tour of my house.**

It's nothing special.

Steve says village houses in the **"original computer game"** aren't so big, though.

I realize this is probably really boring to you. I told you, villagers are boring.

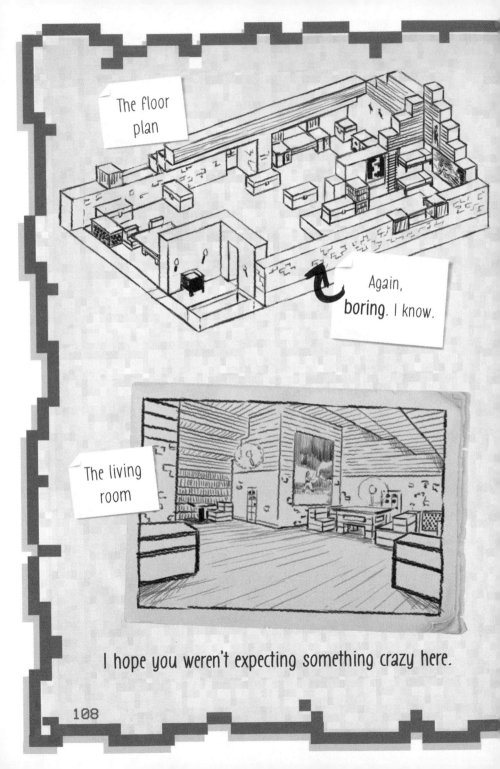

The floor plan

Again, **boring**. I know.

The living room

I hope you weren't expecting something crazy here.

We keep food in the chests on the right. Cook food in the furnaces. Boring, boring, **boring.** Please don't fall asleep.

The kitchen

My bedroom

The top bed is Steve's. He said two beds stacked vertically like that are called bunk beds. Usually kids sleep in bunk beds. Maybe it's **humiliating** for a warrior to be sleeping in such a room, in such a bed, but it's the best we could do. I hope he's not **too angry**.

At first, my parents were going to suggest that he sleep in the living room. But then, that would be similar to making him sleep in the stable, like an animal or something. **Wouldn't it?**

We don't know **Earth culture** at all, so we didn't want to take any chances. We just wanted to be nice. After all, he's the guy who helped us build the wall. Without that huge stone wall protecting our village, we'd be in **a lot of trouble.**

I'd show you my parent's bedroom, but I don't think they'd be too happy about that.

Oh. We also have **a bathroom.**

The bathroom

Again, Steve said in the **original computer game**, village houses didn't have bathrooms. I still don't know what a computer game is. At some point, I'll ask.

Well, anyway, there you have it.

And now Steve is living with us. He's been kind of sad. He just sleeps and sleeps all day.

* * *

Oh, I almost forgot. If you're wondering what happened to that **Mike** fellow . . . **He's in jail.**

The elders decided that was the **best place** to put him, after what he did to that **farmer**.

I'll have to visit him sometime, and find out what his story is. Not now, though—as I said, I'm way too busy with my studies.

* * *

So that's the biggest news. **Two outsiders** are staying in our village for a while. (Not to mention those twenty "**tourists.**") It's happened before. But before, it had always been **noobs**. Not warriors like **Steve** and **Mike**. Usually, the warriors who come to our village don't stay for very long. Just to rest up and trade.

Times are changing.

Part of me is thankful for that. I mean, look at it this way: The only reason I started this diary was because of how crazy things are getting. I wanted to make a record of these troubled times. If I'd started this diary months ago, it would have been the most boring diary in **Minecraftia**. There would have been no point in writing anything. **Months ago, my life was so dull you can't even imagine.** This diary would have gone something like this:

I ate a baked potato. This is how I accomplished it: I grabbed the baked potato (with my hand). Then I moved my arm up (and also my hand). By doing this, I could put the baked potato into my mouth.

A chicken gave me a strange look.

Yes. It looked at me. <u>**With its eyes.**</u> *It's getting too crazy around here.*

* * *

Hurrrrrr.

Even three weeks ago, **that was my life**. So maybe we should thank the mobs, huh? I mean, at least they're making things **interesting**.

After school, I showed my **record book** to Steve.

Honestly, I'm **proud** of it.

Even though every student has one, it's the first item I've ever owned that has a purple glow. Steve **chuckled** as he glanced at it.

"I don't understand," he said. **"What are all these numbers?** Your grades?"

"Grades? Actually, we refer to them as scores. Our skill scores. And this here is our **student level.**"

"So strange," Steve said.

"What's so strange about it?" I asked.

His comment really **hurt** my feelings.

"Never mind."

"Hurrrr! Tell me!"

"It's just, it reminds me of a **computer game,**" he said. **"It's really weird.** I mean, this is obviously a real world, but it still behaves like the game in some ways."

There it was **again**—computer game. Of course, I couldn't resist anymore. I had to ask about that.

Steve paused for a moment, as if not sure **how to explain.**

"Well," he said, "you know about **redstone**, right?"

"A little," I said. "There aren't any classes about it yet, but I kind of know how it works."

He nodded.

"**A computer** is kind of like that. Except way more complicated. You can do a bunch of stuff with computers, such as, um, write to people, and, of course, play games."

Hurrrrr? I had **no idea** what he was talking about. Complicated redstone machines? His world sounds **really interesting.** I bet computer games are really fun . . .

"Also," he said, "even though this world behaves like the original computer game, there are differences." He paused again. "**Minecraft** never had record books, for example. The mobs didn't work together. And, in **Minecraft**, you sat at a desk and used a keyboard and mouse."

Minecraft? Keyboard? Mouse?

What was all this stuff? I asked him more. From what I could understand, in his world, on their redstone machines (or computers) there's a game that somehow copies this world. A game called **"Minecraft."** I don't know why the people of Earth would have a game that simulates our world. **It's a little strange,** right?

After Steve explained, he **glanced** around my bedroom.

"Sometimes, I still can't believe this world is real," he said. "Sometimes, I wonder if maybe . . . maybe I just played too much. Maybe I played so much Minecraft it fried my brain, and this is just some kind of **weird dream.**"

I shook my head.

"If this was just your dream," I said, "that would mean I'm not real . . . and I assure you, I'm very real."

After I said this, the sadness returned to Steve's eyes. I'm not sure why. He nodded.

"Yeah."

The teachers added a new class to our schedules. It's called **Intro to Combat.**

Too cool!!!

When I heard that, I was too excited. Combat is my favorite subject, as you surely know by now. Even though only **five students** this year will become warriors, the elders feel every student should learn at least the basics of combat.

The class takes place in a big field outside the school. When we first arrived in the field, everyone was **pretty excited.**

The training **dummies** were wood blocks and fences pieced together, with **pumpkins** for heads, to resemble zombies. They **weren't anything fancy, but hey,** for a second I began to feel like an actual **warrior-in-training.**

Even better, the class was being taught by an elder. **An elder!** They're the most **respected people in our village.** Besides the mayor, at least. You can imagine how much we students freaked out on hearing this. Apparently, this elder has the **best combat score** in the whole village.

Stump and I looked at each other with **huge grins.**

'It is going to be an **awesome day**,' we thought.

We thought maybe this elder was secretly a **master swordsman**. We thought maybe he'd show us how to dice up mobs into steaks with **just a wooden sword**. We thought a lot of stuff like that.

His name is
Urf.
The **Venerable** Urf.

We thought wrong.
Wrong.

I realized this after Urf took out his wooden sword and began . . . um . . . **"teaching"** us.

"Now, this is how you hold your sword," he said. "This thing here is called a handle. You hold the handle with your hands, see? Like this."

Who doesn't know how to hold a sword? And even I know that's called a **grip**.

I quickly began wondering how much Urf actually knew about fighting. All was revealed, **soon enough**.

"And then," he said, "you swing the sword. Use your arms and swing the sword with all of your strength."

He **clumsily** swung his sword around, <u>cutting the air</u>.

He almost **tripped**. Someone snickered to my left—Razberry.

"Now, I'll swing the sword **at a dummy**," the elder said. "Watch and learn. This is how you **attack a mob**."

He rolled up the sleeves of his **robe**. "I'm really going to dunk this thing."

Urf approached a dummy and swung with a loud grunt. When he connected with the dummy . . . **his sword bounced off** . . . and flew out of his hands. It was hard to see his cheeks, since they were hidden under his huge gray beard, but I could see a hint of red.

"A bit rusty is all,"
he said, picking up the sword.
Rusty, indeed.

Someone behind me coughed. Then Max stepped forward and said: "Um . . . sir? If I may ask . . . what is your . . . combat score? Sir."

Razberry snickered again, proudly.

"**Seven,**" the elder said proudly. "Yes, sonny boy, I've smashed a few **zombies** in my time. I once beat a zombie upon the head with a stick. Rest assured, I'll teach you **all you need to know!**"

"I'm sure," Max said.

"Did that zombie die?" asked a girl.

"Well, no," said Urf. "But it became **very, very angry.**"

Someone **groaned**. There were a few more snickers. **Sighs**. Everyone was thinking the exact same thing I was.

Our combat teacher
has a combat score of 7%. Seven.

Not seventy-five. Not even fifty. <u>Seven.</u>

The best in the village.

Wow.

So **once upon a time,** he almost killed a zombie. Almost.

He was a **noob leading noobs.**

It was hopeless.

The mayor himself might as well have been out here. He's without a doubt the wimpiest villager of all time.

Wait—I shouldn't haven written that. If this diary ever **gets into the wrong hands!**

119

I didn't mean that. No, the mayor is **super amazing** and **awesome** and **fabulous**—he's the <u>coolest guy ever.</u> Yes. That's what I meant.

Anyway, we have a problem. **A huge one.** We need to learn how to **fight mobs**. However, no one knows how. Not even the elders. How can we ever become real warriors if we don't have a **real teacher?**

When it comes to being a warrior, beating zombies with sticks is not what I had in mind . . . For the rest of the class, Urf kept talking about the most basic stuff, like how to swing and how to block. The class seemed to last forever. **Some boy even fell asleep.**

Then, Urf revealed a huge **"secret tip"** at the end of the lesson:

"If there are thirty mobs around you, just **run away**," he said.

He took a swig of water from his water bottle.

"Just run away."

The students were totally silent once more. I myself couldn't believe what I was hearing.

Run away when thirty mobs are surrounding you.

Really? Are you sure?
You mean like, move your legs so you move
away from the mobs? <u>That's brilliant!</u>

Good tip. This elder was a total **nooblord**. Stump and I left the class disheartened. We had to get some ice cream after school. That was the only thing we could think of to raise our spirits.

And it did. In fact, we soon had an **idea** on how to solve this problem. I guess **diamond ore chunk** is just that amazing. Maybe you're thinking the same thing I was thinking at that point. Let me give you another little quiz, then. We need a real warrior to teach us; however, **none** of us villagers are warriors.

So in your opinion, what should we do?

A) Immediately start crying.

B) Ask the mobs real nicely to just stop attacking.

C) Dig down until we hit bedrock and live like dwarves, eating mushrooms and bats.

Or, maybe . . .

. . .

. . .

. . .

JUST MAYBE . . .

. . .

. . .

. . .

(You know what's coming, right? You know. You surely know.)

. . .

. . .

. . .

D) Recruit Steve as a combat teacher?

That's right.

We do have a real warrior in the village. Two, actually. Mike is a warrior as well. Although he's in **jail**.

Hurrrrr. I wonder if the elders would release him if he agreed to help us out?

First, I went to ask Steve about this.

When I went back home, Steve was asleep.

Right now, I'm finishing up my **crafting homework**, trying to ignore his snores.

There's always **tomorrow**.

When I woke up this morning, I checked my **record book**.
My combat score **was up**.

RUNT	
STUDENT	
LEVEL 19	
MINING	1%
COMBAT	5%
TRADING	1%
FARMING	26%
BUILDING	65%
CRAFTING	15%

My crafting score had an even **higher gain**.

That was obviously from my **constant crafting attempts** at night, in my room (sorry Fluffles).

I wasn't too **far behind Max**, then.

This morning, I went out for a walk, and I saw Max in the street. He was looking at his own record book. **I managed to peek at it.**

MAX
STUDENT
LEVEL 24

MINING	7%
COMBAT	6%
TRADING	27%
FARMING	25%
BUILDING	45%
CRAFTING	35%

How is his trading score so high? **Whatever.** He's probably the highest-level student in school. If I keep working hard, I'm sure I'll catch up. Even if I don't, as long as I'm in the **top five**, I'll be eligible to become a warrior.

Still, how awesome would it be to out-level Max? **I can imagine the look on his face!**

* * *

As for Steve, he was still **moping**. He didn't even get out of bed to eat **breakfast**. He took out some bread from his inventory, shoved it into his mouth, **and went back to sleep**.

So I went to go hang out with Stump, Sara, and Ariel. We talked about some **new ideas** for the upcoming mining test. My hope was that by the time I came back, Steve would be up, and we could talk about him becoming **a teacher**.

Well, when I returned, the sun was on its way down, my parents were working in the fields—and **Steve was still snoring away**. It looked like he'd eaten almost an **entire cake by himself**. The last half-eaten slice was lying on the table near the window.

I cleared my throat. Loudly.

Nothing.

He didn't move at all. Then I approached the bed and said:

"Creeper."

He shot up out of his bunk bed. Cake crumbs went flying everywhere. Then he glanced around, his eyes wide, before giving me a dirty look.

"Not funny."

"It wasn't supposed to be."

"Whatever."

He rubbed his eyes. **Yawned. "What time is it?"**

I ignored his question and stepped forward. "What's wrong with you? You've been sleeping all day!"

He only sighed and laid back down in bed. Then he turned away, facing the wall.

Basically, as I came to realize, Steve is "depressed."

He had lost all of his items, all of his **buildings**. What's more, **he had lost his pride**. The mobs defeated him, got past all his defenses. Nothing worse can happen to a warrior than that, I imagine. Not only that, but he's trapped here, in **Minecraftia**. He really misses Earth. For once, it was my turn to be the **strong one**. For Steve.

I marched over to the bed, looked up, and said: "You know, those mobs are going to figure out how to break through our wall sooner or later. Some day, the creepers are going to realize they don't need to bomb us with slimes. They can just **blow up next to the wall,** and that'll be it. **We need you, hurrrrr.** Besides, don't you want to get revenge?"

I thought it was a **good** speech.

But Steve just made a strange **groaning** noise.

"Uuuuugggghhhhhh . . ."

I tried a few more times to motivate him, but he didn't move. He was just **another zombie**. A zombie who sleeps and eats cake. My parents said I shouldn't bother him. They said he needs some **time alone**. That's fine. **I understand.** Besides, he's not the only warrior around.

Tomorrow, I'm going to visit Mike.

I went to the jail today. I spoke with Mike.

He said he'd be **willing** to teach us how to fight. Of course, I asked him if he actually **knew how to fight**.

His response was: "Dude, seriously? Don't you know who I am?"

"Not really . . . **dude?**"

Saying that word—**dude**—it felt awkward. I'd never used it before, and didn't know what it meant. Earth slang, I guess.

He **sighed**. "Well, back home I used to play this game called **Minecraft** . . ."

(Here we go again, I thought.)

I waited for him to continue: **"Urr-hurrrr. And?"**

"And, I was the best warrior ever," he said, **"I was known as Minemaster Mike.** Just get me out of this stupid jail and I'll teach you villagers everything. The mobs won't ever think about going near a village again. The **endermen** will be so afraid, they'll actually start crying just looking at your village. And because water hurts the endermen, their own tears will actually burn them. **See? That's how pro I am."**

"Endermen hurt by their own tears," I said. "Is that even possible?"

Mike **shrugged**. "I don't know. But we're going to find out."

Hurrrrn. I admit, **I really like Mike's attitude.**

Even so, I questioned him further. If he was **anything** like Urf . . .

"If you're so good," I said, looking at him through the iron bars, "then why did you come **running** into our village?"

"**Come on**," he said. "There were like a **hundred** zombies. I just wasn't prepared. I heard that Steve guy got ambushed as well, and he's pretty good, right?"

"**Hurrrrrrrrrrrmmm**. Okay. I believe you. I'll try to convince the mayor to **let you out**."

"**Do your best**," he said. "Just get me out of here, and I'll carry you guys to **victory**. By the way, I really want to talk to Steve. Can you tell him to come down here?"

"That's going to be **tough**," I said. "He's been moping lately. But I'll try."

"Well, you'd better," he said. "Things are getting bad, I guess. I overheard the **guards** talking earlier . . ."

"What did they say?"

"Something about another village, near here. **It was destroyed.** The mobs **overran it**. They didn't have a wall."

Another village . . . destroyed. So that's why those **"tourists"** are here. Mystery solved. Of course, I suspected this the whole time. Maybe I just didn't want to accept it.

<u>And Mike is right.</u> We have a wall. That wall will buy our village some time.

129

* * *

After I left the jail, I sat down next to some farmer's carrot crop. I just sat there for a long time. Thinking. Too much crazy stuff was happening to me at once. **I'm only twelve, you know?** And not only do I have to do homework and do my best in school—I also have to deal with annoying bullies like Max and his best friend, Razberry.

Then, if that wasn't enough, I now have to **cheer up Steve**.

And **free Mike from jail**.

Also . . . I have to convince the elders to let Steve and Mike teach.

So much **to do**.

Why can't things just be **easy**? I'm starting to miss the simple days. The **boring days**. But it's like this: I want to become a warrior. So I can't just freak out when faced with problems, **right?**

Would a **warrior** do that?
Would a warrior just **complain** about
how **confusing** everything is?

My village needs me. I must be strong **right now**. Steve **and** Mike must become our combat teachers. The village needs both of them. You see, there are 150 students; even if I manage to get Steve back to normal, how can he teach that many at once? If Mike helps out, we can split the students into two classes.

Why do I have to do all this stuff, anyway? Why didn't the elders think of recruiting Mike and Steve? Well, I know the answer to that. The older people in our village don't trust outsiders at all. Having **outsiders** as **teachers** . . . it's **unimaginable** to them. Such a thing has probably never crossed their minds. So . . . they're going to be very resistant to my idea.

Sigh. I updated the **"Things to Do"** list in my record book. Yes, the record books can do more than just track our scores and level. **They're handy** little things.

THINGS TO DO

- ☑ DO MY HOMEWORK
- ☑ COLLECT SEEDS
- ☑ FEED FLUFFLES
- ☑ INVESTIGATE THE TOURISTS
- ☐ CHEER UP STEVE
- ☐ GET MIKE OUT OF JAIL

Urrrrggggg.

That's a "**hurrggg**" without an "**h**" sound. It means, I'm so **frustrated**, I can't even properly "hurrggg."

The mayor **won't release Mike**. No matter what. Mike's going to be in jail for a **long** time. The mayor wants Mike to **pay for his actions**. The mayor said if he releases Mike so easily, then others might get the idea that they won't be **punished for any crimes**.

So here's the situation: Steve's **super sad**, and Mike's in **jail**. There's **no way** to get a combat teacher.

Urrrrggggg.

. . .

The mayor did say, however, that he'd be willing to let Steve be a teacher. On one condition. Steve has to **prove** himself. He has to show the mayor and the elders that he has **skill in combat**. Obviously, that's not going to happen anytime soon.

Not with Steve in **depressed** mode.

Sigh.

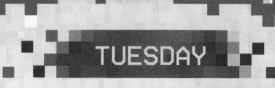

I had to suffer through another boring combat class with Urf **as the teacher.** Of course, Steve's still moping. After school, Stump and I thought of everything we could to **cheer him up.**

Stump baked him a cake. Steve **ate it silently** and went back to **his bed.**

Sara and Ariel even brought him some **ice cream.** Ghast tear swirl.

As expected, he said it wasn't nearly as good as the **ice cream on Earth.**

I **honestly** don't know what to do.
His sadness is **rubbing off on me, so . . .**
I don't feel like writing much today . . .

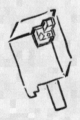

It's **really** late.

I'm writing because . . .

I figured it out.

I finally got Steve back to his normal self.

It was something I'd never thought of, until now. This time, I really have to **thank the mobs**—the spiders, in particular. You see, tonight, while we were sleeping, **another spider** climbed up our house. Somehow, it got stuck on the eave of the house or something. The spider **totally** panicked.

Squeak!
Squeak squeak squeak squeak!

There was a moment of **silence** (perhaps as the spider realized it was totally stuck) until:

SQUEEE-EE-EE-EE-EE-EE-EE-EE-EE-EE-EE-EE-EE-EE-EE-EE-EE-EE-EE . . .

It was—without a doubt—the most annoying sound in the world.

It was more annoying than **Max's voice**. It was more annoying than the kids at school today who asked me **countless questions** about building. As if I'm some kind of **building genius now**. The sound the spider made was **so annoying**, Steve actually jumped out of bed and looked out the window.

"Jeez," he said. "Won't that thing shut up?!"

"I've heard worse," I said. "About a month ago, **spiders carried** some zombies up onto our roof. **Just to annoy us.**"

"You poor villagers," he said. "You guys have to put up with this **every** night?"

"Almost every night." I climbed out of bed. "If it's not the **spiders** squeaking, it's the **zombies** moaning. If it's not the **zombies** moaning, it's the **slimes** oozing around. **Welcome to my life.**"

This was when I had my **idea**.

"And it's your **life**, too, Steve. It's going to be like this **every** night, unless we find a way to fight off the mobs. Make them so afraid, they never leave whatever dark caves they came from."

That did it.
Worked like a charm.

Steve let out a **breath**. His shoulders **sagged**. He **stared** at the floor. Then he took out his **wooden sword** and left my room. Moments later, the squeaks stopped. Perhaps the spider spotted Steve.

135

Squeak?
Cheeeeee—ihhhh!
WHUMP.
Eeeeeehhhhhhhhh—!!
THUD.

And then, silence. When **Steve** came back into my room, he was almost smiling. "Much better," he said.

Now was my time to strike. I knew I had to get him to agree to be a teacher while he was still in **a good mood.**

"So this means you'll be our **teacher**, right?"

"Yeah." He paused. "I mean, I'm stuck in this world, right? I can't do anything about it, so . . . whatever, you know? I might as well help you guys out."

Finally, I thought. Steve was his **normal** self again. But then, there was still a problem . . .

"Now, you have to **convince the mayor** to let you be a teacher," I said.

He gave me a **funny** look. "And how exactly do I do that?"

"The mayor said you have to **prove yourself.** They don't want a **noob** teaching the class."

"Got it," he said. "Tomorrow, tell the elders to meet at the wall, at the north gate. **Okay?**"

"What are you going to do?" I asked.

He smiled, but only slightly. There was a gleam in his eye.

"I'm going to prove myself."

When I woke up, **Steve was rummaging** through my **supply chests.**

"Good morning," he said. "I'm taking some sand."

"What for?"

He gave me a stern look. "Do you want me to be your teacher or not?"

"Okay, okay. Take whatever you need."

"Good," he said. "Then I'm also taking an iron ingot, a piece of flint, some oak wood, and some cobblestone. **Oh, and also, your crafting table. Thanks.**"

"What? What are you going to do with all of that stuff?"

"You'll find out tonight," he said with a wink. "Make sure the elders are there, okay?"

"Hurrrrr. Okay."

After I arrived at school, **I couldn't stop thinking about** what Steve was going to do. Why did he need an iron ingot and a piece of flint? Also, what was the sand for? **I was lost.**

Later that day, I told the elders and the mayor to meet at the north gate. The day seemed to take **forever** to end . . .

Finally, nighttime arrived and I was standing next to Steve at the north gate. Soon, villagers began gathering around us, elders and blacksmiths, librarians and fishermen, and finally the mayor himself. They began talking in low tones. Whispers.

"**Rhurrr**, what is Steve doing?"

"Is he **actually going outside?**"

"At night?!"

"**Hurrrrn**, is he nuts?"

Stump emerged from the confused crowd. **"What's going on, Runt?"**

"**I'm not sure,**" I said. "But I have a feeling we're going to have a new combat teacher soon."

"**Hurrrrr**, what are you talking about?"

"Just watch."

The noise from the villagers grew louder and louder. Steve glanced at them all, then stepped on the pressure plate that opened the wall's iron door. **And then he went outside.** Stump and I scrambled up the wall's ladders to watch what he was doing. The other villagers did the same. **There must have been over <u>five hundred</u> villagers standing on the wall.**

At first, Steve simply stood out there, in the open plains. The sun sank lower and lower. Nothing happened for a long time . . . until mobs appeared in the distance. In the gloom.

Zombies.
Creepers.
Even an **enderman**!!!

Steve had **no armor,** and only a stone sword. Everyone thought he was done for.

Looking at the poorly equipped Steve, you couldn't imagine anything except the mobs turning him into mush.

The creepers came for him first. Steve **leapt in the air** and knocked them back before they could explode. Then, with blinding speed, he cut each of them down. **Strangely, he also collected the gunpowder they dropped.** The elder, **Urf,** wasn't too pleased with this.

"What's he doing gathering **gunpowder?**" he said. "He needs to run away! Those **zombies** are so close! Maybe I should go out there myself and show him how it's done!"

"**Oh,** I can't watch this!" said the mayor, **shielding his eyes.**

A girl was almost crying. "**Those zombies are going to get him! Steve!! Run!!**"

Indeed, the zombies were slowly **shambling** toward him. They were forming a ring around him. **There was no escape.** My heart sank when the **enderman** teleported beside him.

Steve **swung and swung**, striking the **enderman** before it could attack. With an **eerie howl**, the enderman dropped to the ground, <u>**dead.**</u>

Steve bent down to pick up what the enderman dropped. **An ender pearl.** Me being the **noob** that I am, I had no idea why Steve was gathering the items. He should have been focusing on the **zombies** surrounding him, right? Instead, he set my crafting table on the ground. We villagers just stood upon the wall, watching helplessly.

Urf gasped. "**Crafting?**" he said. "Ridiculous! What kind of noob is he? **Why is he crafting in the middle of combat?!**"

Villagers were really **freaking out**. Huge tears, lots of **hurrgggs** and shouts and gasps. Stump and I glanced at each other with wide eyes.

"Steve's acting **really crazy**," said Stump.

I nodded. "**Crazy is what we need right now.**"

The **zombies** were almost on him. Steve set sand and gunpowder on the crafting table. **He was . . .**

crafting TNT.

He set the **TNT on the ground**, next to the crafting table. "**This is for what you did to my base!!**" he shouted.

Everyone gasped at what he did next. He took out his flint and steel, and lit the TNT. The noise from the villagers was deafening. Well, the TNT blast would surely kill most of the zombies, but what about Steve? He was going to die, too—**right? Wrong.**

As the lit **TNT** hissed away, he whipped out the **ender pearl,** and threw it as far as he could . . .

BOOM!!!

The TNT **exploded,** sending **zombies flying.** Most **died** from the **explosion,** of course. As for Steve, he was standing just outside the blast radius. **Untouched.** He had used the ender pearl **to teleport** to safety . . . less than a **second before the TNT went off.** With nothing but a stone sword and some TNT, he had killed a **small army of mobs** . . . without even taking a scratch.

No one could believe it.

I always knew Steve was **good,** but after seeing this, I realized—**the guy's a master.** The **surviving** zombies rose up, bodies smoking. They didn't shamble toward Steve, though. **They were too scared.** For the first time in my life, I saw mobs that were **actually** afraid. When Steve **turned around** to the zombies, as if inviting them to attack, they

ran away *(well, it was more like a slow jog, but still, I'd never seen zombies move so fast before)*.

Steve looked up at all
us villagers on the wall and said:

"That's how we do it on Earth."

I'm a little sad, because my crafting table was destroyed by the TNT. Also, Steve used the last of my sand to craft that TNT, and I'd been saving that iron ingot to make a sword. That flint was for some arrows, too.

I know they're simple items. But I'm poor, remember? The only emeralds I get are the ones my mom gives me to buy lunch. What am I saying? I'd pay fifty emeralds to see Steve do that again. Last night was amazing. Besides, the elders and the mayor agreed to let Steve teach us.

So Steve's back to normal.

Not only that, after Steve's impressive display, the mayor released Mike from jail. The elders are finally starting to warm up to the outsiders. We're cooperating with them.

Of course, Mike also has to prove himself before he can become a combat teacher. We'll see how that goes. Mike's going to fight the mobs tomorrow, just like Steve did.

Now I can focus on my classes and homework, and nothing else. Now that I don't have to worry about Steve and Mike, it's just study, study, study. I'll pass Max. Just wait.

Hurrrrmmm. I really wonder what
Mike is going to do tomorrow.

What **Mike** did was **almost as cool** as what **Steve** did.

A group of witches was outside the village last night. Mike **bought a cow from a farmer** and three iron ingots from a blacksmith. **He also bought something from me.**

Remember that time I **coughed up a slime ball**? Well, I'd stashed it in one of my chests, and Mike was interested in it. As it turns out, he used it to craft a **leash**. He made a bucket with the three iron ingots. It was really weird, but Mike went outside the village wall, tugging a **cow on a leash** and holding a **bucket full of milk**.

Just like with Steve, everyone thought he was nuts. Why would someone go into combat with a **cow**?

Even Steve <u>didn't know</u> what was going on.

And what was up with the milk, anyway?

Of course, there was a reason for all of this. Apparently, the people from **Earth** are really clever.

<u>See, here's the thing.</u> The main attacks of witches are their **poison bombs**. If they can't poison you, they really can't do much. **And milk cures poison.** Just chug a bucket of milk and **all poison** is removed from your body.

Whenever a witch hit Mike with a poison bomb, he drank milk immediately. Then he turned to the cow and milked it super fast. **It was unbelievable.** The witches couldn't really hurt him at all. In this particular battle situation, a cow was **invaluable**.

Tonight I realized that there's **a lot more to combat than swinging a sword.**

Mike cut down the witches, **one by one**. The last remaining witch even started crying.

"Why isn't my poison working?!" the witch cried. "It's not fair!"

"Not fair? Tell that to the zombies who ambushed me the other day," Mike said. **"Go on witch, I'm letting you go.** I'm letting you go so you can tell all the other mobs . . . **this village isn't playing around anymore**. Any **witch** who comes here is going to meet an army of villagers with milk buckets. And if you send **zombies**, we'll replace the milk buckets with lava buckets. We'll have an army of cats waiting for your **creepers**. An army of dogs for your **skeletons**. Water buckets for your **endermen**. And send as many **slimes** as you want. I could use more slime balls."

The witch ran off. The villagers cheered as Mike returned to the village.

"Not bad," Steve said with a grin.

I gave him a thumbs up. **"So cool . . ."** I paused, trying to remember the word, **". . . dude."**

145

Mike smiled. "Thanks."

The mayor approached. "Well done," he said. Then his face became very serious. "Tomorrow, I'd like to have a **special meeting** with you warriors. I have something to tell you. It's about your world, and how you came to exist here. To be honest, **I didn't believe it myself,** until I saw both of you fight. What I've been told . . . **it must be true.** I know that now." Then the mayor glanced at me. "This includes you, **Runt.** I want you to come to my house with Steve tomorrow night."

"What?" I blinked, totally confused. **"Why me? I'm not a warrior."**

"Yes, that's true." The mayor sighed. "Now, Runt, I don't want to be the one to tell you this, but . . ." What **the mayor said next** shattered my heart. **"You are a noob,"** he said. "Combat is not in your future. **I'm afraid you will never become a warrior.** However, I do feel that you have a special connection with outsiders. So please come tomorrow. **That is all."**

After these crushing words, the mayor took off, along with the elders. **Max** and **Razberry** laughed in the distance. They had heard the whole thing. I only stared at the ground . . .

The mayor had said . . . I'm a noob . . . **Well, fine, I'm a noob!!!** I'll **never** become a warrior. The mayor really made me **see the light**. My only purpose is to help the **real warriors** like Steve and Mike.

I am . . . a noob . . .

My life is back to normal.

By "**normal**," I mean it's just studying hard in school and dealing with a few bullies.

I no longer have to worry about Steve and Mike. They're **teachers**, starting tomorrow, and they're building their own houses. More importantly, the other villagers like them. Outsiders used to have a **bad reputation** around here. Before, when one of them walked into our village, everyone would be asking **questions like:**

Who is he going to **cheat**?

What is he going to **steal**?

Why is his head so **fuzzy**?

And . . . what is that funky **smell**?

But everything changed.

Everyone realized some outsiders aren't so bad. They might smell weird, but that's just the stench of **zombie, spider,** and **creeper** guts. They often walk into the village covered in the stuff. In other words, some outsiders are really **amazing warriors**.

I still can't believe how they handled those mobs. Steve took out a small army of zombies using **TNT** and an **ender pearl**.

Mike defeated a group of witches with little more than **a bucket and a cow**. That's how **real warriors** do it.

Even Stump's grandma was impressed. And you can't impress her. You just can't. On her **eightieth birthday**, Stump crafted the coolest cake ever for her. It had an enderman on it. His grandma **really likes endermen**, for some weird reason. When she saw the cake, though, all she said was that the enderman looked more like **a cross between a squid and a bat**.

Hmm.
Actually, maybe she had something there . . .

Well, Stump's crafting ability wasn't so great back then. Which means, back then, my own crafting ability was even wor—um, never mind. I . . . forgot what I was about to say. **Yeah**. Don't you hate it when that happens?

Anyway . . . What's **important** here is Stump's grandma was actually impressed when Steve blew up the zombies and Mike made the witches cry. Everyone was. After that, a lot of people began to think that warriors are pretty **cool.**

To give you an idea: Yesterday, a trader somehow recreated that special warrior **scent**, with something called **"cologne."** He put up advertisements all over the village:

<u>Yeah.</u>

Today, that trader **sold out.**
Can you believe it?
Even my dad bought a bottle.

All of a sudden, it's fashionable to smell like **fermented slime.**
What that means is more students are going to try their best to become
warriors now. So I have **way more competition.** How annoying. My
chances were low before, but now, they're pretty much **zero.** Or maybe
they always were zero. After all, the mayor said . . . He said . . .

He didn't even try to sugarcoat things. If he had, he might have said
something like, **"You need to improve,
sure, but maybe you will achieve
your dream someday."**

Runt . . . you are
a **noob** . . .

Nope. There was no **sugarcoating** of any kind—just the dry, crusty truth. He's right, too. The most **warrior-like** thing I've done is kick a baby slime through a window, and I was scared even then. Even though I've worked so hard, it just doesn't matter. Maybe some people are born to be great. Like **Max**. He's kept ahead of me in levels this whole time, and he probably hasn't worked and studied half as hard as I have.

It's <u>not fair</u>, you know?

<u>So that's it.</u> From now on, I'm just going to focus on being a lumberjack or something. It's a much more **realistic** goal. That means, I'll no longer be writing in this diary. There's simply no more story to tell. It's not like a fairy tale where everything magically works out in the end.

I failed, and that's that.
Good-bye, diary. It's been <u>fun</u> . . .

As if!

Did you really think I'd just **give up** like that? Or listen to what the mayor said? You should know me by now, unless you've just been looking at the **pictures** this whole time. *(I can't imagine why you'd do such a thing, though. My artwork is super terrible.)*

Anyway, this isn't the end. The mayor is just another person I'm going to prove **wrong**. I don't care about what he said. What does he know about combat, anyway? No matter what, as long as I finish in the **top five**, I can choose whatever profession I want.

Some day, the mayor's going to be saying something like: "You? **A noob**? Did I really say something so foolish? No, I always knew you were going to be the best, **Sir Runt**! Please forgive me, sir! Let me polish your sword for you!"

From here on out, it's nothing but studying. No more helping Steve. No more snooping around. **Just studying.** And hey, if I really do fail, well . . . maybe I can try to become a perfume salesman like that other guy. Honestly, that sounds interesting.

Hurrrrr.

I guess it's time to go to the mayor's house.
For that "secret meeting" he was talking about.
I'll update afterward.

It's going to be a special update.

WARNING
The following
entry contains secret
information.

SPECIAL
UPDATE

If you are a **mob** and somehow **stole** this diary, just know that Steve will hunt you down. The only way to avoid a super painful death *(involving cactus and/or lava)* is to return this diary immediately.

If you're a villager, then shame on you for stealing my diary. Also, reading this section is **super against the law**—not just against the law, but **super against the law**. Those were the mayor's words (although I added the "super" part to make it sound more awesome and scary). For anyone else, you're probably reading a **copy** of my diary. That's cool, but just keep the following information to yourself, huh? And, **if you're friends with any mobs . . . don't tell them anything.**

<u>**The warning is now over.**</u> You don't have to be scared anymore. If you started crying reading this, **I'm sorry . . .**

So I headed over to the mayor's house. I didn't want to, but his house always has a lot of food lying around. And basically, he told us stuff. **<u>Secret stuff.</u>** Stuff only the elders know. It didn't start off well, though. I did something really embarrassing.

153

1) Steve, Mike, and I sat down at the **mayor's** dining room table.

2) The mayor looked more gloomy than usual.

3) See the cookie on the table? I ate it. **I was hungry,** okay? And thought it'd be a good idea.

It wasn't a good idea.

4) No one spoke for a little bit. **It was very quiet.** So when I chewed the cookie, the crunching sounds were loud. I guess everyone could hear it. **It was awkward.** I stopped chewing. The **half-eaten** cookie was just sitting in my mouth.

5) The mayor asked me a question. It was something boring like **"How are you?"** I couldn't respond because I had a cookie in my

mouth. But I had to say something, so I tried swallowing the cookie, **ended up choking, and spit crumbs all over the mayor's table!!!**

Thankfully, everyone ignored this. They acted like nothing happened.

Still, there's some bad news. My diary was on the table when it happened. **Open.** Soggy crumbs flew all over the pages. I cleaned it up as best I could, but I probably missed a few crumbs. If you come across any chocolate smears, now you know why. **My apologies.**

Okay, let's focus on the meeting.

You may not fully understand the things the mayor told us. If you don't, that's cool, because **I don't either.**

First, the mayor said, "Runt, I often see you writing in that little diary of yours."

"Yes," I mumbled. I was still angry at him, and embarrassed about **the cookie thing.**

"From now on," he said, "I want you to write down **everything that goes on** in this village."

"**Urrrrrrr** . . . that's . . . what I've been doing."

"Oh, okay. Excellent. Excellent. We'll have a record, then, in case our village ever gets utterly **destroyed.**"

Hurrrrrrr?

Our village? Destroyed? What was he saying?

Mike spoke up. "Um, what's this all about?"

The mayor stirred in his "chair" *(it was really just some upside-down stairs, of course).* "From what I understand," he said, "you two come from a place called **Earth**, correct?"

The two warriors nodded.

"And you play something called **Minecraft**," the mayor said. "A . . . computer game."

Again, more nods. Their faces were showing a bit of confusion by now.

"So what?" said Mike. "We're trapped in the game, right?"

"No, no." The mayor chuckled. "It's not like that **at all**."

Mike shrugged. "I read about people getting sucked into the game, so I just thought, maybe . . ."

"It's **not possible**," Steve said. "There's just **no way** to get stuck in a computer game."

"Whatever," Mike said. "I don't know. Besides, I'd rather believe we're trapped in the game than . . . **the alternative** . . ."

(Naturally, I had no idea what they were talking about. I just sat there and listened, and tried to understand as best as I could.)

"This is a real world," the mayor said. **"Believe it."** He paused for a moment. "I understand computer games in your world **depict imaginary** places. Fantasy lands. However, Minecraft is very different. Minecraft is a crude simulation of this real world, **Minecraftia**."

The warriors glanced at each other, then back at the mayor.

The mayor continued. "Minecraft is a **test**," he said. "Its purpose is to find those with real talent. In short, due to your abilities, you've been **recruited** and sent to this world. The one behind all of this is a **wizard** named <u>Notch.</u>"

"I don't believe it," said Steve. **"Notch?"**

Mike almost laughed. "You're telling me . . . this world is **real**? And Notch is a wizard? From this world? **Can I wake up now?"**

The mayor shot up from his "chair." He pounded the table with his fist. Cookie crumbs bounced.

"This is no laughing matter!" he boomed, and in a lower voice, said, "I'll admit, I didn't believe it myself. Still, after watching you two fight, I realize now that it's true. So listen. Right now, the forces of **Herobrine** are—"

"Herobrine?!"

<u>"Herobrine?!"</u>

Steve and Mike nearly **jumped** out of their chairs.

"Silence!" The mayor pounded the table again. "Look, we need your help. You **Earthlings** obviously know how to fight, so I hope you'll teach the students everything you can. **Herobrine** has been teaching all the mobs, showing them how to work together. The mobs have Herobrine . . . and now, we have you."

(So that explains why the mobs have been getting smarter. Who is this Herobrine, though? I'd never heard that name until today.)

"Of course, **Notch sent others**," the mayor said. "Out there, in the wilderness, are many more **just like** you two. However, they still seem to think they're in the **original game**. So they've done nothing but harass us and steal from us. They won't even talk. Maybe they'll listen to you though. Whenever you encounter them, I'd like you to spread the word." The mayor was referring here to the **trolls, noobs,** and **griefers** who have been **causing trouble in our village.**

(So maybe that explains why they treat us so poorly. They think they're in the original game. To them, we villagers are just . . . um . . . game characters, without feelings.)

There was a long silence.

"How can we go back?" asked Steve at last. "Do you know anything about that?"

The mayor shook his head. **"I'm very sorry,"** he said. "I don't know anything. I'll try to find out for you. I will say that **Notch** is a great man to send you here. That's all for now. **Good night.**"

* * *

Outside the mayor's house, Steve and Mike started talking. I really didn't understand anything they said.

another dimension . . .
parallel universe . . .
alternate reality . . .
blah, blah, blah.

It made **computers** sound simple. Also, I have **no idea who Herobrine** is, but Steve and Mike seemed pretty **freaked** out just hearing his name. And that name does sound a little scary.

Again, I began to question my **decision** to become a **warrior.** Maybe being a lumberjack isn't such a bad idea.

I mean, how could I **fail** at being a lumberjack? Trees don't **move**. Or **bite** you. Or **spit fireballs**. Or sneak up on you and hiss and blow up half your house when you're least expecting it.

Basically, tonight, I learned:

1) The outsiders were sent here by a **wizard** named <u>Notch</u>.

2) Some **bad guy** named <u>Herobrine</u> is the reason the mobs are getting smarter.

3) When you're in a **quiet place** with other people, don't eat something crunchy.

<u>Just don't.</u>

Today, Steve and Mike taught the **Intro to Combat class.**

As I originally assumed, the teachers split the huge 150-student class into two **75-student classes.** Stump and I are in Steve's class.

Steve went over the **basics,** and **I mean the real basics,** like how to position yourself properly in combat and how many swings it takes to kill a spider with a wooden sword.

Still, Steve's mind was **wandering all day.** Sometimes, he would just stop talking in the middle of a sentence:

UM . . . WHAT?

Steve was **obviously** thinking about what the mayor said last night. I forgive him because my combat score went up **7% today**. I'm all the way up to **level 26!!!**

RUNT
STUDENT
LEVEL 26

MINING	15%
COMBAT	12%
TRADING	1%
FARMING	37%
BUILDING	68%
CRAFTING	19%

In other news, a lot of kids **asked** me about building.

"Runt, can you give me tips on raising my building score?"

"Hey, will you teach me after class?"
"How much do you charge?
I heard one emerald per hour?"

It was amusing, at first, but now it's just **annoying**. And that girl Sara . . . she's **way more friendly** to me, recently, than she used to be. What, all I have to do is ace a building exam and suddenly people like me more? **Why?** I don't get it.

Max is still as **annoying** as ever, though. He had to remind me of what the mayor said at least once:

"How's it going, noob? By the way, is that an official profession in our village? **Noob?**"

And then: "Actually, Runt, after seeing you take care of Steve, I'd say you're more like a **nanny.**"

Which led to: "**Head Nanny Runt,** I'm just wondering how I'm doing. I've swept the school floor. I've scrubbed it and mopped it and even polished it with a slime ball. I hope to become an awesome nanny like you. Please tell me how I'm doing."

It's **only** going to get worse, too.

Once Max learns the mayor asked about **my diary**, he's going to explode. I'm assuming he'll try something like **putting boogers** in my diary . . . *(He did that to Stump's record book the other day.)*

This morning, while Stump and I walked to school, we saw an outsider. **A warrior, I guess.** Stump tried talking to him. All we could get out of him before he took off was that his name was **Joe**.

He probably didn't have much to say anyway. He looked like a warrior, but he was probably a **bad one.** I mean, **gold armor** is for noobs. Both its durability and protection are terrible.

Well, after school, we saw Joe again.

At first, Stump and I just ignored him while he walked down the gravel road. Then an **idea hit me** so hard, it was like an arrow shot from a bow enchanted with **Punch II.** I was literally knocked back by the awesomeness of it. I thought of a way to raise my level.

This warrior-noob, Joe, could actually be useful.

You see, trading is a factor in our **student levels**. It's one of our scores. It's my worst. So if we could make a successful trade with Joe, our trading scores and levels would go up. I explained this to Stump. Then we ran to my house and rummaged through my item chest for some **random item we didn't need.** We found a pair of leather boots in good condition.

Then we ran back to **the noob.**

HELLO!

HI THERE.

WANNA BUY THESE BEAUTIFUL LEATHER BOOTS?

> **NO**

That was it—just **"no."**

Not **"I'm sorry, but I don't need them,"** or "some other time, maybe," or even a somewhat courteous **"no thanks." Just "no."**

Then he **walked away!!!**

Stump **sighed**, said he had to get back home and do his homework, and took off as well. I realized that trading wasn't as easy as I'd thought. **Whatever.** I still had faith in my idea. I wasn't giving up just yet. However, I needed a **strategy.**

I thought for a moment, then caught up to that outsider noob, and said:

> **BUY THESE BOOTS. THEY'RE SUPER COOL, I PROMISE.**

> **NO, THEY'RE NOT.**

Man, this guy . . . Didn't he know that these are good **leather boots?**
I guess he just wanted to show off.
Soon, I thought of another way.

**BUY MY BOOTS!
BUY THEM NOW!**

DUDE... SERIOUSLY,
GO AWAY.

Hurrrrr. So brute force **didn't work.**
Clearly, I needed to try something else.
Another idea hit me.

**PLEASE, SIR, WOULD
YOU BUY MY BOOTS?**

KID, I'LL GIVE YOU AN EMERALD IF YOU GO AWAY.

No! No way!

I wasn't going to go away until this cheapskate coughed up at least two emeralds, maybe three. **Joe** strolled off along the gravel path. My mind was racing.

"**Imagine this,**" I said, running after him. "What if—"

"Imagine me walking away," Joe said, interrupting my sales pitch.

"Wait! Don't imagine!"

I grabbed him by the shoulder.

"**Listen,**" I said. "Do you see those plains?"

Joe stopped walking, and gave me a blank look.

"Yeah."

"Do you know what's beyond those plains?"

"No."

"**A desert,**" I said. "A huge one. Hot. Dry. No water for at least **3,000 blocks.**"

"So?"

"So what if you're walking in that desert some day, and your boots give out? **What will you do then?**"

He paused for a second.

"Um . . . **I'll craft new ones?**"

"And what if you don't have a crafting table on you?" I asked.

"I'll craft one?"

"And if you don't have any wood to craft a crafting table?"

"I'll gather some?"

"And what about leather?"

"I'll find some cows?"

(**Sheesh** . . . couldn't he see that I was **trying** to make an **honest** emerald, here?)

"But there are no trees in the desert," I said. "No cows for **leather**. You'll be **walking barefoot** across hot sand with no way to craft new boots. That's why you should always keep an exlra pair on you at all times. A warrior told me that."

Suddenly, Joe's eyes lit up.

"Omigosh!! You're right!! I never thought of that before!! Do you still have those boots?!"

I gave him a grin **flashier** than any diamond.

"Right here, **my friend.** For the low, low price of just **three emeralds,** these quality boots are yours."

Ten seconds later, there was a tinkling sound as three emeralds fell into my hand.

"Thanks a lot," he said. **"You're a cool kid."**

"No problem."

And at the same time,
I thought: thank you.

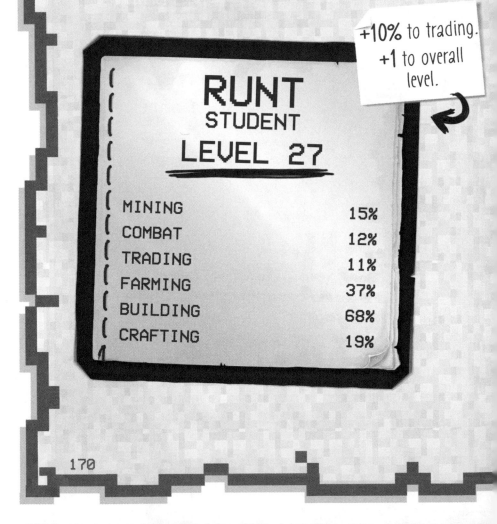

+10% to trading.
+1 to overall level.

RUNT
STUDENT
LEVEL 27

MINING	15%
COMBAT	12%
TRADING	11%
FARMING	37%
BUILDING	68%
CRAFTING	19%

Well, I really did have to work for it. A part of me feels **guilty,** though. Perhaps I cheated him slightly—I could have asked for two emeralds.

It was for the greater good, though. Besides, if he ever ran into a really skilled trader, he might have paid ten or more for the same item.

In a weird way,
I saved him money.
I'm such a nice guy, huh?

My arms are like **dead slime** again.

Mining class was **really tough** today. We've been digging a downward staircase tunnel as part of a project. We've been working on it since the start of school. I never mentioned it before because there was nothing interesting to say about it. Until today. Today, we finally reached **bedrock.** For those of you who don't know, bedrock is the indestructible layer at **Minecraftia's** core. **Too cool!**

Then the teachers hit us with some **surprise** news. There's another **test** tomorrow. A mining test this time. We barely have any time to prepare for it. The teachers just said, "Good job on the tunnel. Tomorrow you're having a test and here are the rules."

The rules are pretty simple. As before, there are **seventy-five teams**—two students per team. Naturally, Stump and I are partners.

- The goal is to **gather ten diamonds.**
- The **first team** to do this gets first place, the second team second place, and so on.
- Each student will be given an **iron pickaxe.** If someone is caught bringing in any extra tools, they will be **disqualified,** along with their **partner.**

More than a few students **complained.** Finding diamonds depends **more on luck** than skill.

Even so, the teachers argued that proper mining techniques will increase a **team's chances of winning.** The faster a team digs, the faster they'll find diamonds. Teams must work together and come up with mining strategies.

Mining this deep is **really dangerous.** ⬅

We could run into a **lava pool** . . .

For this reason, all students will be given a bucket of water and a potion of fire resistance. **Now,** those are great answers for lava, obviously . . . but what about mobs?

But don't worry, I'm not scared. I've got a combat score of 12% now. That's good, right? I'll take on endermen with my fists if I have to. *(I'm lying. I'm actually super scared.)*

The mining **test** began shortly after everyone trudged down to the bottom of the tunnel. **Potions,** water buckets, and iron pickaxes were handed out.

Then we were off. The seventy-five teams scattered in different directions.

Stump and I dug and dug.

I swung that pick as fast as I could—as I swung, **I imagined Max's face on every block of stone.** Imagined him laughing. Imagined him **calling me a nooblord**, a noobmuffin, a head nanny. It gave me all the **strength** I needed.

Stump eventually argued that we needed to split up. He was right. We could cover more ground that way.

(Yes, that was the best plan we could come up with. Look, we're not mining geniuses. **Not yet.***)*

After we dug far enough away from the other students, I began mining my own tunnel, while Stump continued mining the original. Finally, I was **super far away** from everyone else. When I stopped mining, I couldn't hear anything, no sounds of other students digging, nothing, just **eerie silence.** And I wondered if maybe I wouldn't be able to find my way back. I'd placed torches on the walls to provide direction, but still . . . **What if I was lost?**

I kept mining anyway, not wanting to fall behind.

Chunk, chunk, chunk.

My pickaxe broke another block of stone. And then, a brilliant white light hit my eyes.

Diamond ore.

My heart started pounding. Sweat poured down my face. I mined all the stone around that diamond, and realized . . . **It was a double vein.** Normally, a diamond vein will yield three to eight diamonds. But this was two diamond veins, right next to each other. There were **eleven diamond blocks** encased in that stone. This single discovery was enough to complete the test.

Here's the bad news. *(There's always bad news with me, huh?)* In all my excitement . . . I had stopped **paying attention** to the durability of my pickaxe.

Chooonk!!!

It broke as I finished mining away the surrounding stone. Well, I really panicked then. Here I was standing before **the biggest diamond vein ever,** and I had no way to mine it. Just my luck. Seriously, this kind of stuff always happens to me.

Obviously, I had to go find Stump. I had to find him before his own pickaxe broke. I had to find him before someone else found this vein and stole it. **Wait.** If I just left this vein sit here, surely someone would spot it, and take everything. I had to find Stump, yet I couldn't leave. And if I shouted, trying to get Stump's attention, others would hear.

I mean, what if I just bellowed, **"Hey! Stump! I found a huge diamond vein! Come here! Quick!"**?

Every student within 2,000 blocks would be on me like an army of chickens running to a mountain of seeds. **I'd never been so nervous in my life.**

Then, a few seconds later, I heard someone approaching. It was probably just Stump, I figured, but I wasn't going to take any chances. **I had to conceal my find.** I went into my inventory and realized when you mine stone, it turns into cobblestone. I had no natural stone. The only way to make natural stone would be to bake cobblestone in a furnace. I could have made a furnace, of course, with my huge amount of cobblestone—however, **someone was approaching.** I simply didn't have that much time.

That was why I began placing cobblestone around the diamonds to try and hide them. I was so nervous and frantic, I even placed an oak block instead of cobblestone. I did this right before that person approached. **It wasn't Stump.**

It was Razberry.

→

"Have you seen Max?" he asked. "I'm lost."

"No," I said. "I haven't seen him at all." I was angry at myself for just blurting that out. I should have said something clever like, "Yeah, I just saw him over there! 5,000 blocks that way! You can't miss him!"

Razberry sighed. "Well, have you found any diamonds yet?"

"None," I said. "Just coal, coal, and more coal. No diamonds around here."

My heart sank as he peered at the cobblestone behind me.

"Hurrrrrrr, hey . . . what's that cobblestone doing there?"

I gave the cobblestone a quick glance.

"Oh, that? That's just . . . a natural cobblestone formation!"

"A natural cobblestone formation?"

"Yep. They're pretty rare. What, don't you know?"

"No, I've never heard of . . . wait, what's up with that wood?"

Great, I thought—and came up with some pathetic explanation.

"It's part of an underground tree," I said.

Razberry stepped closer. He got right up next to me, still staring at the cobblestone.

"An underground tree? That's **really weird,** don't you think? Are you sure that's what it is? Maybe you'd better take a closer look."

I did, turning around, pretending to be amazed.

"Wow, I can't believe it, but that's definitely what it is," I said. "Wow. I mean, wow."

"Yeah, it's pretty cool," said Razberry.

"Yes. It's so great. I'm so . . . **amazed!** Totally, absolutely . . . amazed!"

Thankfully, Razberry isn't too bright. He actually believed me.

"Me, too," he said, "Okay, I'm going to go look for Max now."

"I think I remember seeing him down that way," I said, feeling relieved.

"Thanks. Bye."

He took off, and a moment later, so did I. I soon found Stump swinging away at his tunnel; my heart felt a chill as he lifted his pickaxe over his head. It couldn't have had much durability left . . .

"Stop!!!" I hissed.

He froze, then turned around with a blank face.

"What?"

"Come here. Quick!"

After Stump mined away the cobblestone, and saw those diamonds, he didn't say a word. He just kept swinging away.

What luck.

His pickaxe broke on the last block mined.

Ten minutes later, we were back at the huge chamber where all the teachers were. We handed the diamonds over, one by one, **grinning like** . . . something that grins **a lot.**

We won.
We got first place.
Again.

Stump started jumping up and down, and gave me a **huge high five.** "Yeahhhhh!!"

We aced a building test, and now we just aced a mining test. I was about to out-level Max. **I'd no longer have to worry about anything**—my future as a warrior was all but certain. **And then—**

A teacher stepped closer to me.

"Please show me your inventories."

"No problem," I said, and showed her my inventory screen, as did Stump. (Steve said you can't do that in the original game, but hey . . . this is **Minecraftia**, not a game.)

"Hurrrrrrr! What's that?" she said. **"A diamond pickaxe?!"**

At first, I didn't understand what the teacher was saying. Then it hit me. There was a diamond pickaxe in my inventory. **Enchanted. Enchanted with Efficiency II.**

Stump gasped. "What the creeper?! How did that get there?!"

"Give me that!" the teacher snapped. There were a bunch of murmurs from the other teachers around me. **What . . . was . . . happening . . . ?** Why did I have an enchanted diamond pickaxe?

"It's not mine," I said, handing over the tool. "I . . . I don't know how it got there!"

"So this is the real Runt," said the head teacher. **"A cheater!"**

"You've got it all wrong!" said Stump. "I was with him almost the whole time! That pickaxe isn't—"

"Enough!" the head teacher snapped. "Both of you are hereby disqualified! You have failed this test!"

"It's a trick!" I shouted. "Someone set us up!"

"No more lies, young man. Now I'm wondering if maybe you cheated on the building test as well."

I heard someone snickering in the distance. Two people, actually. And right then, **it was all so clear . . .** I recalled Razberry stepping closer to me in my tunnel. He had tricked me into turning around and looking at the cobblestone so he could slip that pickaxe into my inventory. I'm sure that was what happened. Max's family is rich. He probably asked his parents for emeralds and bought that pickaxe yesterday. **How stupid am I?**

There I was, thinking I was so clever for tricking Razberry . . . But it was Razberry who had tricked me. Max and Razberry walked up and handed the teachers ten diamonds.

"Show me your inventories," the head teacher said. They did. Both of their inventories were empty, **of course.**

"Well done, you two!" Max winked at me before walking away with his best buddy.

Well played, Max. Well played.

I didn't go to school today. I said I was sick. I am.
Kind of.

I'm **mentally** sick. **Emotionally sick.** Most of all, I'm sick of being picked on.

I stayed in my bedroom all day, **reading a book** called *Orggor, the Zombie Pigman Creeper Golem.* It's a fun series. Something to take my mind off everything.

TAKE THAT, YOU NOOBS!

ARRG AGRGG

He's 35% creeper,
25% iron golem,
25% zombie,
15% zombie pigman—
and 500% awesome.

At some point, Stump **barged** into my room. I didn't look up from my book.

"**Rhurrrrrg.** I just want **to be alone** right now."

"And do what?" asked Stump.

"Read."

"Hurrrrr. I don't blame you. **That's a good series.** But still, there's another test on Monday. A trading test this time."

"**Great,**" I said. "Maybe we'll get **disqualified** for that one, too."

Stump shook his head. "Listen, I've thought of a way to **come back.** We can ace that trading test even more than we did the building test. It'll put us back in the game. **Trust me.** Let's think of it as our next **secret project.**"

"**Not interested,**" I said. "Anyway, can we talk about this later? Orggor is about to destroy a Nether Fortress and I want to find out how he does it."

"He just smashes everything. **Nothing fancy,** just smashing. Can we discuss **Project X2** now?"

I glared at him. "**You just spoiled the book!**"

"You're acting just like Steve did when the mobs blew up his base," Stump said. "**Hurrrrg. Whatever.**"

Before I could respond, he left my room. I turned back to my book. What's the **big deal?** I thought. What, can't I feel **sorry** for myself? **It's over.** Max is probably level 50 by now, and we didn't get any points for the mining test. Probably that one kid Pebble is a higher level than me now and he's the **biggest noob of all time** . . .

Still, I couldn't help thinking about Stump. What was this **"Project X2"** he was talking about? What crazy idea did he cook up? I couldn't help myself. I had to find out. **Pigman Golem** could wait.

Before I knew it, I was **running** out of my house.
I saw Stump in the distance, walking slowly away.
"I'm sorry!" I called out, sprinting to catch up with him.

He turned around and smiled.

So the trading test is on Monday. We have **two** days to prepare.

According to Stump, **the rules for the trading test are like this:** there's no school Monday. All **students** must go around the village and attempt to trade with adult villagers—blacksmiths, fishermen, and so on. Teachers will observe students from a distance, to assess their trading skills. **Students are allowed to cheat the adults.** In fact, it's **encouraged**. Also, no one in the village knows about this, except for the teachers and students. If a student manages to **cheat** an adult, the teachers will come up and tell the adult what's going on. They'll even give those we cheat **extra emeralds** to make up for it.

Sounds pretty cool to me.

And then, Stump came up with a **master plan** to ace this test. That means—Project X2 has officially begun.

Actually, we renamed the project to "**Project All Eggs In One Basket.**" The reason for that name change will make sense to you soon enough. However, I'm not going to write about the exact **details** of our secret project until we attempt it. Again, this is to protect us, in case someone steals my diary.

I will say it requires a large amount of cactus and bone meal.

The bone meal isn't a problem. My parents have a ton of it lying around. They use it to make their crops grow faster. They're farmers, **remember?**

So I can probably sneak a bunch of it from the chest in the kitchen. **The cactus, though . . .** that's tough. Looks like we're going to have to go into the desert tomorrow and harvest as much cactus as we can.

If we get caught traveling so far from the village, things are going to get real bad. Whatever.

It's all or nothing.

All eggs in one basket.

To make a long story short, **we got some cactus.** As soon as the sun came up, we ran to the desert. I brought water bottles, Stump brought cakes, and we harvested cactus until our inventories were full.

Later on, I took a stack of bone dust from my parent's item chest in the kitchen. Just one stack. There were seven total. No one will notice.

And now, I'm signing off for today. **It's crafting time.** Oh. **One more thing.**

I've come to realize . . . I need a **plan B** in case I don't make the **top five.** That backup profession is **perfume salesman.**

You see, I'll be able to get revenge that way. If I fail, I'm going to make **Eau de Noob** and put Max's face on the advertisement.

EAU DE NOOB
(MEGA-NOOB)

So tempting . . .

FOR **NOOBS** AND **CHICKENS** ONLY 3🪙

Today was it.

My last shot at making the **top five.**

There was no school. All of us students were **wandering** the streets, looking for **someone** to trade with.

Stump and I already had someone in mind.

Leaf is his name. He's an old guy.

A blacksmith. **A bit cranky.** His beard is so bushy, it covers half his nose. And his eyesight . . .

it's the worst.

In addition, he's one of the best blacksmiths in our village. He's got lots of items for trade.

All of the above is why he chose him.

He was our target. **The perfect target.**

Soon, he would become our **victim.**

Soon, **Project All Eggs In One Basket**

would be unleashed upon a cranky old man who could barely see. I didn't feel sorry for him, though. To me, he was just a tool that I was going to use to improve my grades. Besides, the teachers would reimburse him, after he got cheated.

And oh, was he going to get cheated! I knew even then that our project couldn't fail.

It was just too good. **Too crazy.** I was glad to have a best friend like Stump. You see, we used that cactus to make **"cactus green."** We sat by the furnace for hours, watching the cactus cook down into what is basically green dye.

Then, the cactus green was combined with bone meal to make a brighter **lime green dye.**

Now, maybe you're wondering, "Why would someone want to make lime green dye?"

 ## Allow me to explain.

As I've mentioned before, outsiders sometimes come into the village to cheat us. The **most common scam** is trying to pass off **green seeds as emeralds.** No villager has ever fallen for that, of course. It's pretty easy to tell the difference.

I'm sure you'll agree.

Here's your typical noob trying that scam:

"They're just really small emeralds! **I swear!"**

Well, Stump thought of a similar scam,
except better.

Seems all that time he's spent crafting cakes finally paid off.

Here's how it went down.

I walked up to **Leaf**, and asked to **trade.**

I offered an emerald for **two iron ingots.** I even held out an emerald to show the blacksmith **I wasn't fooling around.** "See? Shiny emerald! Real!"

Well, the blacksmith thought I was a **total noob.** One emerald for two iron ingots is a really good deal for the person getting the emerald. **The poor blacksmith** had no idea what he was actually about to get.

Pro tip: it wasn't an emerald. As soon as the blacksmith looked down at his iron ingots, **I switched the emerald . . .**

with a dyed **lime green** egg.

Stump's parents are **bakers**, so his house had a huge supply of eggs. The trick was pretty convincing. **Especially to the blacksmith,** who couldn't see very well.

Of course, I asked to trade more of my **"emeralds"** for more iron ingots, and the blacksmith smiled. He thought it was his **lucky** day.

"How many more do you need, sonny?" Leaf asked.

"How many do you have left?"

"Ohhhhh, let me see here. About fifty, I'd say."

I smiled. "Then fifty it is!"

The blacksmith peered at me **suspiciously.**

"Say, where'd a kid like you get so many emeralds, **anyway?** Found the motherlode, **did you?** An emerald cave?"

I shrugged. "If you don't want to **trade**, I'll just go somewhere else. Sorry for bothering y—"

"N-no no," the blacksmith said, not wanting to ruin his "good deal."

"Tell me what you need, and ol' Leaf here will fix you right up."

And so a total of **fifty iron ingots** was traded for **twenty-five green eggs.**

"Anything else you need?"

"What else have you got?" I asked.

"How about this fine bucket?"

"**Sure,** I'll take it."

"And how about some wool?"

"Sounds good. What else?"

"Hmm. How about this **fine—**

"I'll take it."

"You didn't even let me finish speaking," he said. "How do you know if you'll want to trade for it?"

"Listen," I said, "just give me everything you have. **Everything.**"

And so a mountain of items was purchased with **tons of dyed eggs.**

Stump had to help me carry them all, because my inventory was overflowing. I figured the more items we cheated out of the old blacksmith, the more **impressed** the teachers would be.

Then we ran out of the blacksmith's place before he caught on and chased us with a stick or something.

Two teachers soon **rushed** over to us.

"**Wow!**"

"Amazing work!"

"How did you **come up** with that?!"

"By the way, Runt, we discovered that the pickaxe wasn't actually yours. We'll get everything sorted out. **Sorry.** This has never happened before. Do you have any idea who could have done this?"

"I have an idea," I said, but I didn't even care about the mining test anymore. Max wasn't an **issue** anymore. My record book soon updated with an **unbelievable sight.**

RUNT
STUDENT
LEVEL 45

MINING	25%
COMBAT	12%
TRADING	100%
FARMING	37%
BUILDING	68%
CRAFTING	32%

Boom!!!
Victory secured.

But this incredible recovery doesn't mean I'm a genius.
This was all **Stump.**

I've learned many things in the past few weeks, but what I learned today . . . **it's the most important.**

If you have a best friend who treats you really well—who never turns their back on you—well, **never turn your back on them,** no matter what. And if your **best friend** happens to be a creeper, I don't know what to say. **I can only imagine how awkward that must be at times.**

Explody! It's been so long! Give me a hug! No? Okay, how about a handshake? Oh, um, right. Never mind.

Is this really happening? We're going to become warriors.
It's almost a certainty.

Tomorrow, I'm going to tell my parents about this.
I don't know how they're going to react.
Wish me luck, huh?

We **built** a cave near the school today.

From a distance, it looks like a **huge pile of cobblestone** just sitting in some empty field. **Nothing special.** But pure awesomeness is contained within.

THE
SECRET CAVE
LOLOL

It's for combat training. We can practice how to fight in **darkness,** which warriors sometimes need to do. When you take away the torches, it's pretty dark in here.

196

It's big enough to hold **seventy-five students.**

Now, you're probably thinking something like, "Why did Runt make a picture of a dark cave? **It's not like anyone needs a picture to imagine a cave."**

I agree.

The above picture is, without a doubt, the most boring picture I've ever made. Some cobblestone walls? Some dirt underneath? All of it barely visible due to the lack of light?

Well, this is a **diary about my life**, and not everything in my life is exciting.

Furthermore, this drawing of a simple cave illustrates what lengths we're going to become better villagers. We built a cave in the **middle of our village to train.** That's hardcore, huh?

197

Beyond that, if you're ever talking to your friends about boring pictures, well, just direct them to this **picture**. Maybe some day one of your friends might say something like, "**Dude, I was reading this one book,** right, and it had some boring pictures . . ." And you can be like, "Dude, I know of a book that has **a way more boring picture** than whatever book you're talking about. Dude."

(By the way, am I overdoing the "dude"? I just want to sound like an **Earth** kid.)

And your friend will be like, "Dude, no way. The book I just read was literally titled *The Most Boring Book Ever Written*." And you can be like, "I'll bet you five emeralds." And he'll be like, "Okay, you're on." And you'll whip out this **diary,** show them my cave picture, and your friend will be like, "Okay. Wow. **Wow**. Just . . . wow. Now that is the most boring thing I've ever seen. I give up. You win. You win. Here. Take my emeralds. Please. Just take them. I feel so sorry for you, for reading that boring book . . . even if we **HADN'T** made a bet, I'd give you emeralds out of sheer pity."

(This is basically an easy way to get free emeralds.)

(Unless you're one of those Earth people. Steve said Earth people don't use emeralds, but **shiny metal things** and pieces of paper and plastic cards. I find that **really strange**.)

Anyway, today during combat class, in the secret combat cave, every student had to fight a zombie while everyone else watched.

When it was **my turn** to fight, it was so dark.
All I could see was the **zombie's shadowy form.**
I filled in the details with my **imagination**.

I imagined the **zombie's sunken black eyes.**
I imagined the zombie's mottled green skin and old stinky clothes.
An image of the zombie appeared in my mind . . .
Actually, at first, I imagined **a steak** instead of the zombie.
I was so hungry.
I focused again, trying to picture the zombie before me . . .

Urrrrrg!

(When a villager forgets to make an "h" sound during a "hurrggg," you know
he's annoyed.)

I just **couldn't stop thinking** about food!

I hadn't had breakfast or lunch, and all the hard work we did in class that morning made me really hungry. I mean, since **eight this morning** I've been running, jumping, and swinging a sword.

That kind of stuff really **drains** your hunger bar, you know?

Well, it didn't stop there. After picturing **big juicy steaks,** my imagination really started to soar . . . I **finally** did picture a zombie. At least, it had **a head, arms, a body** . . . but something wasn't **quite** right . . .

a cake **zombie?!**

I shook my head.
Blinked.

I had to snap out of it.

My hunger was out of **control.**

Surely you've imagined a cake zombie before, too, right?

When you were **really hungry?** You have, right?

Please tell me I'm not alone here.

Okay, there we go. That's more like it.

So there I was in the secret combat cave, fighting a zombie. I felt so nervous, because **one hundred forty-nine other students** were watching me, and so was Steve, out teacher.

Any little mistake I made, everyone would see, and laugh at me. I had to fight to the best of my ability. I couldn't do that while imagining cake zombies, and if I kept thinking about that, who knows what I'd think of next. **A cookie golem?**

I swung in the zombie's general direction.

Swish!

The blade of my wooden sword cut through the air before hitting the mob. **Clunk.** I gripped my sword tighter and stepped back, thinking about the situation—I was in serious warrior mode.

Now, a single zombie isn't much of a threat. **They're slow**—you can dance circles around them, if you're brave enough. *(I'm not.)* They also **stumble** around like a pig on stilts. *(I don't know what stilts are. I'm just quoting Mike here.)*

And even if a zombie does hit you, the **damage** isn't very high—probably about as bad as that old **Urf** guy hitting you with a stick or perhaps a carrot.

Plus, they never try to protect themselves. Zombies just come at you in a straight line like noobs to signs that read "ZOMG DIAMONDS HERE."

Even so, it would be foolish to get careless when fighting a zombie. A single zombie can still be dangerous. Even if the damage they deal is pretty low, the attack will still knock you back.

<u>Imagine this:</u> you could get knocked back by a zombie, into another zombie behind you, then the second zombie would knock you back AGAIN, this time off a cliff, and you'd land in a river . . . and you'd think, **"Wow! I survived that!** I didn't take a scratch from that! I got knocked off a cliff, landed in a river, and didn't take any falling damage at all, as if I were a cat! How lucky am I?!" And then you'd see that the river is actually flowing toward a waterfall. **And a lava lake,** down below . . .

(If that ever happens to you, I'm really sorry. Please be careful when fighting zombies.)

A zombie dance party.

Plus, a zombie can **"call"** another zombie, spawning a new zombie nearby. *(How zombies spawn other zombies is quite mysterious, but more than that, it's highly annoying.)* The new zombie that the first zombie calls can call its own zombies. A single zombie can quickly become a small **army of zombies.** The zombies will multiply, one zombie after another zombie, as each new zombie **calls more** zombies. At first, it will only be one zombie, but it will quickly become a **zombie party** with many zombies doing . . . whatever things zombies do. If the zombies are on top of a cake, they'll start dancing around.

<u>Top secret info:</u> I wasn't joking about zombies dancing on cake. **See for yourself.** If zombies step on cake, they'll begin bouncing around like crazy! **Perhaps cake** could be used to **protect** our village somehow. I'll consult Stump on this, since he's the **baker.**

Anyway.

These were just a few things I learned in combat class so far.

I tore myself from my thoughts for a second, and studied the zombie's movements.

Hurrrrm.

Actually, it wasn't moving **AT ALL.**

I swung my sword again.

"Haaaa!!"

And hit the zombie **on top** of the head.

Bonk!

I swung with such force **the blade bounced off,** and I staggered back.

My mind was **racing** the whole time.

Let's go over some **numbers,** shall we?

A wooden sword deals **two and a half hearts** worth of damage with a single strike. A zombie's life force is equal to ten hearts.

That means, four swings with a wooden sword should kill a zombie, because 10 divided by 2.5 equals 4.

However, zombies have a small amount of **natural armor.** Two armor, if I recall correctly. So what is that? A total of 8% damage reduction? I can't remember, but what I do know is that dropping one requires **five hits** with a wooden sword. *(I've never killed a zombie before. I'm just a really good student who listens ALL THE TIME.)*

But, if you use a leap attack and swing while you're moving downward, you'll deal more damage with a critical hit—that's big boy stuff. I decided to finish the zombie off with such an attack. I guess I just wanted to be cool. **To show off.** Everyone was watching me, right? So I had to do something flashy. **It'd make Max jealous.**

I moved back then charged forward and **jumped in the air, sword drawn . . .**

Oh, and I also made another ridiculous battle cry.

"Hiiiiiaaaaaaaaaaaaaaaaaaaa!!"

I was going to make a **perfect** attack. This leap attack was going to be so cool, so powerful, it would be too hard to make a picture of. If someone ever tried making a picture of the leap attack I made, and put it into a diary, the picture's **awesomeness** would simply make the diary explode. I don't want to endanger you, so I'm not going to include the picture here.

Just use your imagination. Imagine me, Runt, your favorite villager warrior kid, flying through a dark cave, sword held in both hands like a **ninja**, screaming louder than a poo screamer.

Awesome, right?

That zombie had no idea how much damage he was going to receive! I was going to show all the other kids who were watching me how cool I was. I was even going to impress Steve, our teacher—who, of course, was also watching me. I was—

OOOF!!

I smashed into the zombie before I even managed to swing my sword. I didn't even swing my sword . . . I just slammed into the zombie like a bowling ball slamming into a pin. I bounced off the zombie's body and flew into the air, and landed on my back. My sword flew in another direction, clattering on the ground. The whole cave erupted into laughter.

How . . . annoying.

I remained there on the cavern floor for a moment, just breathing.

"Lights!" shouted Steve.

Some girl whipped out a torch, then another kid did the same, until the whole cavern was lit up.

"Can you tell me," said Steve, **gazing** around at the students, "what Runt did wrong just now?"

Max snickered. **"Everything?"**

A few others laughed as well. Stump reached down and helped me up. "Runt just forgot to time his attack, that's all," he said.

"That's right," said Steve. **"In combat,** timing is everything. Swinging or jumping at the wrong time can mean the difference between **winning or losing** a battle. You don't want to bowl into a zombie, if you can help it!"

More laughter.

Not from me, though.

The only thing that came out of my mouth was a big sigh.

It seems like some things **never change.**

Even if I've out-leveled almost everyone by now, I'm still not getting much respect, **just laughter . . .** There was, of course, a very good reason why everyone laughed so much. It turned out I wasn't actually fighting a zombie.

It was . . . ummm . . . Uhhh . . . Errrrr . . .

First, before I tell you . . . please don't laugh at me, okay?

Everyone else laughed at me, and if you also laughed at me, I'd be the first villager to produce ghast tears. *(Maybe that wouldn't be such a bad thing, though. I could sell them.)*

Okay, the zombie was . . . **a <u>practice</u> dummy**.

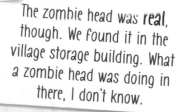

The zombie head was **real**, though. We found it in the village storage building. What a zombie head was doing in there, I don't know.

It wasn't even a good dummy. As everyone stared at the dummy, the dummy's right arm—which was a piece of fencing—**fell off.**

A **poorly crafted dummy, with only one arm.** I was defeated by this.

How pathetic . . .

"Steve? When will we fight **real** zombies?" asked Sara.

"Yeah," said a boy named Pebble. "Real zombies move, you know? And . . . **don't have arms that fall off.**"

Steve sighed.

"I know," he said. "I know. I'm . . . working on it. You guys need to fight real mobs, not . . . this," he said, glancing at the dummy.

"I just don't know how we're going to get real zombies into the village safely. **The elders will never agree to that.** And they'll never agree to letting me take you guys outside."

"There has to be a way," said a boy named Mound.

"I'll think of something," said Steve. He paused. "All right. That's all for now. Class dismissed. **Have a good lunch.**"

Of course, after most of the students cleared out of the cave, Max just had to come up and say something.

"Wow, Runt," he said, looking me up and down. "I didn't know noobs could fly. I sure learned a lot this class."

Razberry grinned at me. "Watch out for those practice dummies, huh? They are **REALLY** dangerous!"

The two snickered again and took off.

Steve gave me a pat on the back.

"Don't **worry** about it," he said. "It happens. Even to the best of us."

"Yeah, sure," was all I could say.

I didn't let it get to me, though. I don't consider myself a kid anymore. Even if I'm still twelve, the village has a lot of problems and I have to help solve them. The biggest problem being the **army of mobs** that may attack our village again. There haven't been many attacks recently, but it's probably because they're planning.

An army,
just waiting to strike.
An army controlled by someone named Herobrine.

Who is Herobrine, anyway? A wizard like Notch? Or some kind of **freaky monster?**

I had a dream that **Herobrine** lived in a big castle, and I helped attack that castle and ran my sword through Herobrine himself.

But I don't even know what he looks like. So **in my dream,** I imagined Herobrine to be something crazy.

Herobrine

Pumpkin pie hands?!

No, no, my dream wasn't **THAT** crazy.

Besides, there's **no way** Herobrine looks like that. If he did, all it'd take to defeat him would be sending Stump after him. *(Stump can eat even more food than I can, and that's saying something.)*

Jeez . . . I've got to stop thinking about food. My stomach is rumbling, and my food bar is almost empty. I need to go get something to eat. Otherwise, **I'm going to start eating this diary.**

Bye for now.

Okay, so, as established yesterday, there's a <u>new</u> problem.

Even though we have Steve and Mike teaching us the ways of **monster slaying**—and even though we have a cool little **secret cave**—the practice dummies can only go so far.

Dummies don't move like real mobs. They don't **attack** like real mobs *(I'm thankful for that.)* And they certainly don't smell like real mobs. *(I'm super extremely enthusiastically oh-my-Notch thankful for that. I still can't eat apples due to the whole rotten apple plus sweaty feet smell a wet zombie gives off.)*

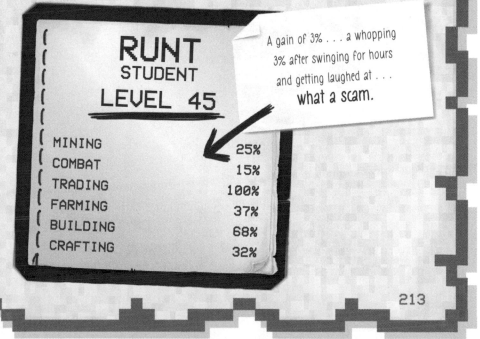

```
( RUNT
(   STUDENT
(  LEVEL 45
(
(
(  MINING        25%
(  COMBAT        15%
(  TRADING      100%
(  FARMING       37%
(  BUILDING      68%
(  CRAFTING      32%
```

A gain of 3% . . . a whopping 3% after swinging for hours and getting laughed at . . . **what a scam.**

What I'm saying is, **we need real mobs** if we want to push our combat scores higher. **As you can see, my combat score needs serious improvement.**

So after school today, I had an idea.
An even better idea than the furnace house.
I'm fully <u>confident</u> in this!

I'll explain.

You see, we need real mobs, **right?**

But the big problem is, mobs usually travel in packs. Go beyond the wall at night and you'll get mobbed by a mob of mobs. **MOBBED.**

A mob of mobs!

Plus, how can you contain a single mob? **Leashes won't work, from what I understand.** And asking a few zombies to please just stroll into the village so we can beat on them won't work. Therefore, I came up with an ingenious solution.

I'm going to craft . . .
A monster box.

It's like this. Mobs spawn in dark places, right? So why not create an area—pitch black, no light—for the purpose of spawning mobs?

You might call me crazy, but today I began working on my **monster box.** I built it on my family's house, on the side of my bedroom.

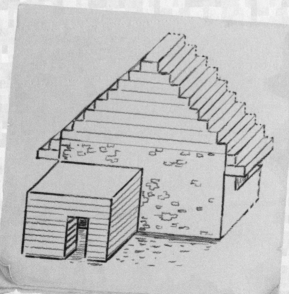

Of course, my dad came over to see what all the fuss was about.

"Whatcha doing, son?"

There was no way I was going to tell him I was building **a room for mob spawning,** so I had to come up with an excuse. A lie, in other words.

"I'm building a **mushroom farm,** Dad. It's for a school project."

He glanced at the structure, shrugged, even smiled.

"A mushroom farm, eh? That's my boy! Make sure to put slabs on the floor so mobs don't spawn."

"You bet."

He nodded. "I'll let you get back to it, then."

After he walked off, **I felt a little sad.** First, I had just lied to my dad . . . Second, I remembered, I'm going to have to tell him my dream of becoming a warrior.

He'll be **crushed.** I know. But it's for the greater good. All the farms in **Minecraftia** won't do us any good when the mobs finally figure out how to break the wall and an army of **zombies comes pouring in.**

And we can't expect old man Urf to fend off the hordes with his stick. We students, the young generation, we're the only hope this village has. Steve wants real mobs, so we'll get real mobs.

Then I put a sign next to it. Hopefully, no one will mess with it.

MUSHROOM FARM
DO NOT DICTURD

I sealed the monster box up as soon as my dad was out of sight.

It's kind of scary knowing mobs might spawn right next to my bedroom, while I'm sleeping, just a few blocks away.

Actually, knowing my luck, maybe nothing will spawn at all. For now, I'll just wait and see what happens. I should probably **talk to Steve and Mike** about this, but after thinking, I decided against it.

It'll be a little **surprise.**
In the words of Cow the Cow . . . Tee hee.

Nothing spawned in the **monster box** last night.
I'll just keep waiting.

* * *

Meanwhile, I'm the **second highest** level student at school.

Even if my actions and failures come with a few laughs, I'm no longer "noob" status, but "not bad," "pretty cool," or even "that furnace house kid" or "green egg kid." All that really means, though, is that kids ask me to help them with their homework.

At this rate, I'll soon overtake Max.

MAX
STUDENT
LEVEL 54

MINING	55%
COMBAT	17%
TRADING	78%
FARMING	36%
BUILDING	61%
CRAFTING	77%

He can sense it, I think. That must be why he's been **bullying** me more, calling me more names, and just being **more annoying** in general. Today, he kept showing off his record book in class. He angled it in my direction **so I could see it.** Gave me a big wink.

Trading and building are pretty much the only areas I beat him in. I guess he just wanted me to know he's number one, and it's always going to be that way.

In brewing class, a boy named Rock asked Max if he could help him with his homework.

Max glanced at him, then at me, and said: **"I don't know. I'm pretty busy these days."**

Then Max whipped out his record book—**suuuuuper slow**—so everyone could see.

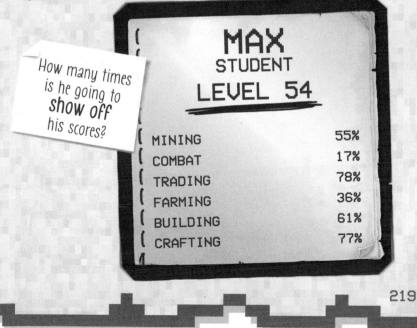

How many times is he going to **show off** his scores?

MAX
STUDENT
LEVEL 54

MINING	55%
COMBAT	17%
TRADING	78%
FARMING	36%
BUILDING	61%
CRAFTING	77%

"I need to work on my combat score," Max said. **"It's so low."**

The truth is, Max's combat score is the highest out of all 150 students. He was just bragging.

Then our brewing teacher told us there was an extra brewing class today, after school. Attendance wasn't required, but anyone wanting some additional practice with potions could come.

Max whipped out his record book **AGAIN**—and again,

reeeeallyyyy sloooow . . .

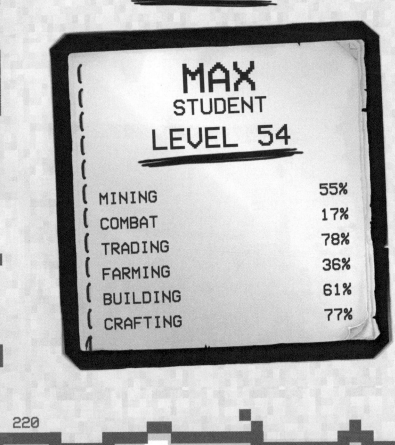

MAX
STUDENT
LEVEL 54

MINING	55%
COMBAT	17%
TRADING	78%
FARMING	36%
BUILDING	61%
CRAFTING	77%

He had to work on his mining, he said **quite loudly,** because it just wasn't high enough.

The only student with a higher mining score than Max is **Pebble,** and that's because Pebble comes from a family of miners.

Okay, Max. We get it. **You're the best.**

So annoying.

During combat class, Max approached me.

"You know," he said to me, "I don't know how those teachers found out about that **pickaxe.** Do you know how many **emeralds** I spent on that thing?"

"Go away," I said.

"As you wish, **Head Nanny Runt.** I'll just go sweep the floors and you can inspect them later and tell me how I'm doing."

Head nanny? I'll show you head nanny, I thought. I practiced as hard as I could; swung my sword with all the strength I had. My practice dummy shook from the repeated blows.

Then I glared at Max.

Max **thrashed** his own dummy, and **returned the dirty look.**
I couldn't see his eyes, because of his glasses, but his eyebrows were
furrowed. **He must have been angry.**

We kept chopping at our dummies and
glaring at each other for a while.

I remembered all the times he bullied me, all the things he said—
"head nanny," "noob," calling my cat Fluffles "Danger Kitty," sabotaging
us in the mining test—**and my anger just exploded**.

With a huge leap, I dived at my dummy, trying to perform another
critical strike. This time, I didn't forget to swing my sword.

I hit with such force, the dummy was nearly knocked over. One of its
arms flew off, as did its head.

I gave Max another angry glare.

Steve clapped nearby.

"Nice job, Runt! I saw that! Your first critical hit, **huh?**"

RUNT
STUDENT
LEVEL 47

MINING	25%
COMBAT	20%
TRADING	100%
FARMING	37%
BUILDING	68%
CRAFTING	32%

After class, I found my score was up.

Max was looking at his own record book, **shocked.** His combat score had only risen 2%—from 17% to 19%.

My score was now higher than his. I showed him my record book.

"Maybe you can teach me a thing or two about fighting, Max,"
I said. "My combat score is so low."
He gasped. "Hurrrrrrrrrrrr!"

FRIDAY

This morning was kind of **weird**.

Max wasn't **in class** today. It was the first time he didn't show up at school. I began to wonder if what I did yesterday really **hurt his feelings** or something.

Then after school, as I was walking home, **I ran into him** in the street.

"Listen," Max said. "**I want to talk to you.**"

"Leave me **alone**," I said, and walked past him.

"**Hey,**" he said, "just listen, huh?"

"**Listen to what?** Head nanny? Noob master? Fluffles the Danger Kitty? Or maybe you're going to tell me more about **poo screamers.**"

Almost before I finished my sentence, he stepped closer with a serious face and said: "I was **suspended** from school today."

For a second, my brain couldn't process what had just been said.

Suspended?
Max had been suspended from school? As in, he was <u>no longer a student?</u>

"**Only for a day,**" he said. "Today."

"What happened?" I asked.

"Someone **ratted** me out," he said. "Pebble. That miner kid. **I bought that pickaxe from his dad,** you see. So his dad came to school and told the teachers I was the one who bought it."

"I don't get it," I said.

"**My only guess** is I must have made him angry when I was showing off my scores the other day."

"Still," I said, "**why would Pebble** do that? I thought you guys were kind of friendly?"

Max removed his glasses. His dark eyes seemed even darker.

"You really don't get it, **do you?**"

I blinked. "Get what?"

"**You and I,**" he said, "**we're the top dogs.** Everyone wants to take us down."

Another blink.

Max put his glasses back on. "When you went **nuts** in that trading test," he said, "and got a perfect score, what do you think happened?"

"Um, **my level increased?**"

"Yeah, and so now **you're the second-highest-level student,** right?"

"Right?"

"And that means **Pebble,** who was originally the second highest, is **now the third.** I'm sure I don't have to tell you what that means."

"Try anyway," I said.

"It means I'm no longer the one you have to worry about, Runt. **You've made a lot of enemies,** buddy boy."

Enemies . . .

What Max was saying suddenly **became so clear.** At least twenty students, as far as I know, want to become a warrior. Probably more than that. The problem is, only five can become warriors.

"Some of the kids are really **jealous** of you," Max said. "You've drawn **a lot of attention to yourself**, doing so well in those tests. In fact, I might have done you a favor by **preventing** you from getting first place in that mining test."

I tried not to get angry when he said this. "Explain."

Max nodded. "I overheard Pebble talking with some of his friends the other day," he said. **"They were talking about you."**

"And what did they say?"

"They said you're a **noob**. Said you have **no business** being a warrior. Said you becoming a warrior will **endanger** this village. Pebble even said he's going to do **anything** he can to prevent you from becoming one."

"This is crazy," I said.

"It gets worse," Max said. "Pebble said . . . his father is going to do something during the next mining test. **Something about a cave-in.** They're going to try to hurt you, Runt . . . **or worse.** Now, I know, I've pulled a lot of pranks on you. But I've never done something like that."

"I can't believe this."

"Me either." Max sighed. "You know, the kids who graduate **in the top five** . . . they'll not only become warriors. They'll have the **option of becoming elders** later, too. A lot of families here realize this. It's a **power** struggle. They're thinking about the future."

"Why tell me all of this?" I asked.

"Well, it's like this. If those other kids hate you so much, how do you think they feel about me? Maybe they're planning to hurt me, too. A cave-in accident, who would know? I don't exactly like you, Runt, **but I respect you.** You've got skill. And I think, for the good of this village, you need to become a warrior. I say we form a **partnership**. Work together. You, Stump, and me. It's us against them."

I didn't know what to say.

After all we've been through, now Max wants to team up?

"What about Razberry?" I asked.

Max shook his head. **"Nah.** I've already talked to him. He's not concerned about his scores. His dream is being a **baker**, not a warrior."

"Hurrrrm. Well, I'll think about it," I said, which was a lie. There was **no way** I was forming a partnership with Max. At least not until he proved that he could be **trusted.** And apologized **a billion times.**

And anyway, I didn't know for sure if what Max was telling me was true.
Maybe it was just another one of his tricks?

This morning, I met up with Stump and we went for a walk around Villagetown. **I told Stump everything** Max said.

While we were walking through the streets, we kept hearing adults talking about a **"tree."**

"Did you see the tree?"
"Wow, it's **so big!**"
"A dark oak, eh?"
"It wasn't there **last night!**"

I glanced at Stump, **who just shrugged.** Neither of us knew anything about this **"tree."** We walked up to **Leaf,** the old blacksmith, **and asked him about it.**

"Some kinda tree growin' in the east," he said. **"Real big feller, too.** Go see fer yerselves!"

Of course, Stump and I **zoomed across** the village and **climbed up the east wall.**

We were expecting the kind of **giant tree** found in fairy tales and storybooks. But from the wall, it looked more like **a sapling.** There haven't been many monster attacks these days. I guess the adults have been bored, and a dark oak tree growing in the distance is **"big news."** It's not even that strange that a big tree like that is growing

230

there. There's a forest to the east. Probably the forest is just expanding. Forests do that, don't they?

Whatever.

All day today, I couldn't stop thinking about what Max said. Are the other kids really so **jealous** of me?

Stump's the seventh-highest student as far as level goes—**are they jealous of him, too?**

"Even if Max is joking," Stump said, **"he's right, you know?"**

"Right? Right about what?"

"You've out-leveled almost everyone," he said, "but you shouldn't get too confident. Things always change, and . . . when you feel too sure about yourself, you get careless **and make mistakes."**

Hmm.
Stump's got a point there.

But then, me feeling **too confident?** I doubt that will ever happen. Even when **I'm doing my best,** I still doubt myself . . .

In other news, nothing has spawned in the **monster box.** No sounds have come from it, at least. It's just an **empty room** sitting on the side of our house. I put a **mushroom** in there just in case my dad decides to check. If he saw that there weren't any, he might get suspicious.

Later, Stump, Sara, and I got **ice cream** again. Sara forced me to try **Creeper Crunch. Yuck.** It was **really bad.** Not just really bad, but I'd-rather-eat-mushroom-stew-with-apple-chunks bad. If you're ever in **Minecraftia**, and get ice cream, I suggest either **Ghast Tear Swirl** or Diamond Ore Chunk.

I finally told my dad about my dream of becoming a warrior. As I expected, he was **crushed.** Actually, I'm not sure he even believed me. Later, I overheard him talking to my mom. They think I'm just going through **a phase.** They think I really want to be a farmer, because I made that "mushroom farm." **If only they knew the truth . . .**

In the evening, **I went over to** Steve's house. Steve and Mike have been building their own houses in their free time. They live **close to the wall,** on the edge of the village.

Steve's house is on the left. Mike's house looks more like a **small castle** than a house. And what are those **weird** face-looking things in the walls? I decided to check Mike's house out, after I visited Steve.

Steve's
house

Steve's house was pretty basic.

After I said hello, I had to find out where that **ladder** went to.

"Hey!" Steve said. "Where are you going?!"

I zoomed down the ladder **before he could stop me,** my curiosity getting the best of me. It was an **underground tunnel.**

Steve's house and Mike's house are **linked by this tunnel.**

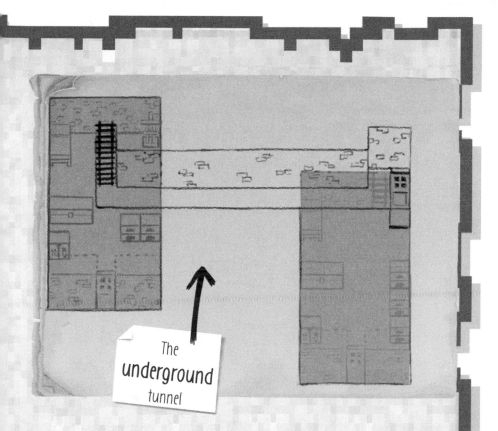

The **underground** tunnel

Steve **explained** it all to me after he climbed down the ladder.

If mobs ever overran one house, they could **retreat** to the other house through this tunnel.

A **pretty cool idea**—villagers never did that.

Next, I checked out Mike's house.

It had an **iron door**, just like Steve's.

But I still had **no idea what those things** in the walls were.

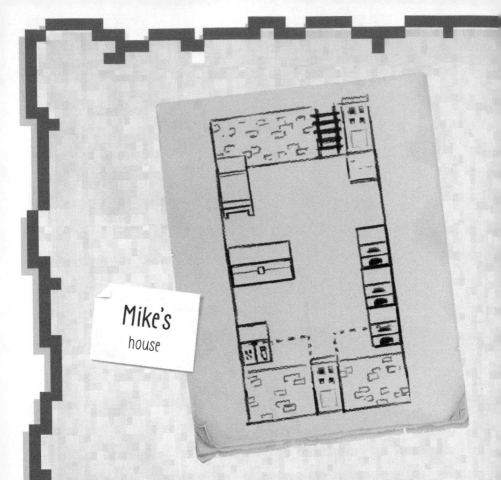

Mike wiped his brow after I stepped in. He was hunched over a furnace, **smelting some ore.**

"Hey, Runt. **What's up?**"

"**Nothing.** I just want to check out your house. Is that cool?"

"Sure."

The door in the back led to the **tunnel** connecting to Steve's house. But I was more interested in the **ladder going up.** Did it have **something to do** with those faces in the walls?

236

I started climbing the ladder. Strangely, there was a kind of attic. It wasn't big enough for a person to stand up in. Those things in the walls were also visible. Red powdery trails went to each of them.

That was redstone, right?

There was a pressure plate on top of his house.

Of course, I wondered what it did, exactly. So I walked toward it . . .
I heard Mike **call out** from down below: "Hey! Don't step on that—"

But it was too late.
Click.

Mike climbed up after me and sighed. **". . . pressure plate."**

Lava poured out everywhere, burning the grass. He stepped on the pressure plate again, and **the lava stopped flowing.**

"Sorry," I said with a pained look.

Mike approached the edge of his house **and looked down.** Then he glanced back at me. **"You owe me a new sign."**

* * *

I didn't have time to cause any more damage. Steve and Mike had to leave to meet with the mayor again.

"**Great,**" I said, "I hope he has more cookies."

Steve shook his head. "**Sorry, Runt.** The mayor said only we can go."

Mike nodded. "**It's nothing important, anyway.** We're just going to instruct the builders on how to **upgrade defenses.** Stuff like that lava fountain."

They **took off,** and I headed back home.

Things were **so quiet** these days.

So boring.

No new mob attacks.

No mention of Herobrine.

Yet whenever I saw the mayor, Steve, Mike, and the elders, **they all looked so serious.**

It was like the **calm before the storm.**

Something was going on. But hey, they didn't want me to be a part of it, so whatever. **I didn't feel like** training anyway.

I'm burned out.

I went back home and read.

I was back at it again.

I had two combat classes today, and the whole time, I was **ducking, tumbling, leaping,** and **swinging** away.

It's been **so boring**.

No new mob attacks.
No mention of Herobrine.
Nothing spawning in my <u>monster box</u>.

The **biggest news** has been that single dark oak tree.

Even Max hasn't bothered me much. Gone are the days of him calling me the King of Noobs. Today, he greeted me with a simple **"Hello."**

And I think he's right about Pebble. Whenever I walked past Pebble and his friends, they glanced at me and fell silent.

Dude, at least call me some names or something.

<u>SOMETHING.</u>

Someone . . . somewhere . . . DO SOMETHING.

Then, after school, something happened.

More
trees

More trees in the east. Everyone in the streets was talking about it.

Okay, okay, I really should have been a lumberjack, I guess. I will become a lumberjack. If those trees are seriously the **biggest threat** to our village, then so be it. I will take down those trees and cut them and shape them into planks.

URG. How boring, right?

As I stood on the east wall, **looking at the trees,** I noticed Steve and Mike in the distance, **along with the mayor.**

If I just walked right up to them, they'd probably **stop talking,** just like Pebble and his friends. So I snuck up on them like a creeper, hid in some grass, and **listened to their conversation.**

"**Fire,**" said the mayor. "We need fire to **burn those trees.**"

"**I wouldn't suggest getting too close to those trees**, though," said Mike.

"What about **flaming arrows?**" asked Steve. "Is that possible?"

Seriously?
<u>Seriously?!</u>

They were having a hushed and **serious conversation**
about removing trees?!
And they haven't told
<u>**me anything about it?!**</u>

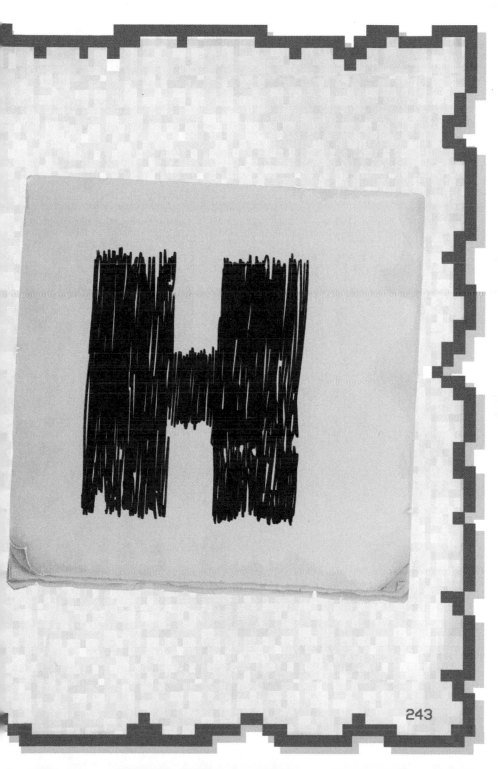

I just couldn't **believe** they wouldn't tell me about something **so small** as this. Trees are growing near the village.

Oh dear.
I was angry.

I walked up to them.

"**I'll admit, I'm no lumberjack,**" I said, "but I've swung an axe a few times before! **Come on guys, let me in on this!**"

Steve, Mike, and the mayor looked at each other.

Steve stepped forward. "Runt," he said, "**it's nothing major, okay?** We just don't want to get you involved. We want you to focus as much as you can on your studies."

"**That's right,**" said the mayor. "Runt, remember when I said you would never become a warrior? **I was simply testing you.** I wanted to see how you would **react.** And you didn't let my words affect you in any way. In fact, **it strengthened you.** That's how a real warrior would react. So please, **go back home** and do your homework. Don't let your level fall behind."

Mike nodded. "**Just a few trees, buddy boy.** Nothing we can't handle."

Buddy boy?!

I wondered who started using that phrase first, Max or Mike?

Whatever. I know something is up with those trees. **But what?**
I listened to them, though, and went back home.

That was when I heard it.
A weird noise,
coming from the monster box.

To be continued . . .

Hi Yeah, I KNOW
Whatta cliffhanger, right?!
Seriously. Hurrrr . . .

I had to pause somewhere, though.
The story picks right up in book 2:

Cube Kid is the pen name of Erik Gunnar Taylor, a writer who has lived in Alaska his whole life. A big fan of video games—especially Minecraft—he discovered early that he also had a passion for writing fan fiction.

Cube Kid's unofficial Minecraft fan fiction series, *Diary of a Wimpy Villager* came out as e-books in 2015 and immediately met with great success in the Minecraft community. They were published in France by 404 éditions in paperback with illustrations by Saboten, and now return in this same format to Cube Kid's native country under the title *Diary of an 8-Bit Warrior*.

When not writing, Cube Kid likes to travel, putter with his car, devour fan fiction, and play his favorite video game.